INDIGO JOE

When middle-aged Joni is introduced to the debut song from a new band topping the charts, 'Indigo Joe', by her music-loving son, she realises the lead singer is that of a boy in her class when she was a primary school teacher in her twenties. She reflects to this time when troubled-but-gifted Jonah entered her classroom. It was September 2001, and his possible prediction of 9/11 left him as a boy she never forgot. Whilst in her class, he uncovers his potential, but it's intuitive Jonah who encourages her, set in her ways and alone, to seek the courage needed to find the happiness she has today.

ABOUT ME

I am first and foremost a scriptwriter with a master's degree in scriptwriting and a strong portfolio of scripts, of varying lengths and genres, seeking a break into industry.

This is my first to convert from a script to a written story. The script was originally written many years ago, being my second to complete. It has evolved over time, undergoing many edits.

It is special to me as I have worked in schools for over twenty years, the majority as a teacher. Its aim is to capture the dedication and passion of those within the profession.

'Indigo Joe' is dedicated to anyone who has ever given their heart and soul to teaching.

As my first story to publish, I also dedicate this to my daughters, parents, family and friends - with the most wholehearted thank you to those that have read my work, and believed in me, every step of the way.

This story is solely my own ideas and uses only fictional characters.

Full script, songs and my writing CV are available on request.

Contact me: camillecrosswriter@gmail.com

ONE

Joni stands by her front door with an expression of amusement that she is always the first to be ready to leave on busy mid-week mornings. She is in her mid-forties and stands as a woman of pride, content with her achievements in life. She is wise for her years but youthful in demeanour. She is casual smart in dress with a well-maintained short hair style. She puts on her coat and grabs her bag.

Her husband rushes towards her, taking her by surprise. He is a tall man, clean shaven and has a short, neat haircut. He is smartly dressed in a suit and tie, straightening the tie as he walks. His happy nature and warm smile cause her to smile in return, with a look of deep love in her eyes. He returns the affection in his gaze.

"I must go. I'm running a little late," he states with calmness in his tone and an accent that reflects modest roots.

He peers up to the stairs and walks towards them.

"Boys, have a good day," he shouts up. Some muffles come from upstairs in reply. He shakes his head in amusement.

He kisses Joni on the cheek and smiles lovingly at her.

"Stacey, no rushing. Just drive safely," she whispers, making clear eye contact with a tone he knows to pay attention to.

"I will. See you tonight, honey," he replies with reciprocated eye contact that portrays he appreciates her concern for him. They kiss. Stacey then opens the front door and goes to leave but pauses to address her.

"Oh, I just saw on the news that tomorrow is the twentieth anniversary of 9/11."

"It's been twenty years?" Joni instantly replies with some shock.

Stacey nods.

"We'll catch the news tonight," Joni informs him.

"See you then, Joni."

"See you tonight," she smiles warmly to him.

Stacey closes the door behind him. Joni walks to the bottom of the stairs and looks up.

"Jake. Luke. Time to go," she shouts.

Two boys head down the stairs with a noticeable contrast between them in appearance. Jake is the eldest at age fourteen. He is tall and thin with brown, messy hair. Luke, aged twelve, is shorter and stockier with blonde, neat hair. He carries football boots.

1

"It's my turn for music in the car, remember," Jake announces clearly. "Oh, and no headphones. Your rule, mum," he mocks jovially.

Joni shakes her head to herself.

"Yes, no headphones. Why do I make these rules?"

Joni, Jake and Luke all walk out of the house. Jake and Luke grab their bags as they leave, and Joni closes the door behind them.

They walk to the car parked outside their house and open the car doors. The house is detached, well looked after and has a good front area for parking. The street is that of similar properties, in a typically wealthier London style.

Inside the car, they all put on their seat belts. Jake is in the passenger seat and plugs his phone into the sound system. Luke is in the back seat with the football boots on his lap. Joni nods towards the boots.

"Is it football in PE today, Luke, or are you training tonight?" she asks.

"It's PE, so no, you don't need to pick me up," he replies.

Joni nods with a happy expression to this that is instantly interrupted by a loud blast of music. She jumps in surprise.

"Jake, that's too loud."

Jake turns down the volume with an amused smirk.

"No headphones," he coyly mimics his mum. "We're going to be social and share our music with each other."

Joni glances back at him with a smile that has an undertone of a warning. He smiles cheekily and she smiles back with a giggle. They hold a gaze that connects them.

Joni starts the car and moves it to the end of the driveway, looking to see if it's safe to pull out. It's a moderately busy road and cars are passing. She waits.

"Anyway, mum, as a music lover yourself, you might want to hear. This is going to be the next big band," Jake informs her.

"Who are they?" Joni asks politely, lacking interest and keeping her eyes on the road.

"This is Indigo Joe," he states.

Joni takes her eyes from the traffic and looks straight at Jake, totally startled.

"Who?" she asks, directly and sharply.

Jake pauses by her reaction, frowning at her with intrigue.

"They're called Indigo Joe," he replies with an expression that asks why she would react as she has.

"Indigo Joe?" she questions, frozen as she awaits his answer.

Jake studies her, puzzled. She puts on the handbrake and faces Jake.

"Are you okay?" he asks in confusion. Jake looks to Luke who is also looking at his mum with interest. Both boys pull an expression to each other to show neither knows why she would react like this.

"I once taught a little boy who called himself, and his band, that. A little boy called Jonah Huckle," Joni states flatly to explain.

Jake gasps in shock.

"Mum, the singer is called Joe Huckle," he replies with some surprise.

"I taught him when he was six years old, but I guess he'd be in his twenties now," she tells them with shock in her voice.

Jake types on his phone and then shows it to Joni.

"That's him now. He's in his twenties," he says, holding the phone closer to her.

Joni takes the phone from Jake and studies it. Her eyes widen and she opens her mouth in genuine shock. She then looks up at Jake with a smile creeping over her face.

"Oh, my. That's him. That's the little boy I taught."

"You're sure?" Jake asks dubiously.

Joni shakes her head in disbelief.

"I'm sure. Oh, I'll never forget him."

Joni stares at Jake and laughs in disbelief, passing him back his phone.

Joni looks back at the road, sees a space and pulls out. They all drive along as Jake starts the song again, from the beginning, and he softly sings along to it. Joni continues to shake her head in disbelief.

> I want to live in new build house
> With a roof terrace overlooking the sea
> Own a brand-new fitted kitchen
> And a huge widescreen cinema TV…

"What's the song called?" Joni enquires.

"This song is called 'All My Life'. It's their first single. They released it recently," Jake answers. He then turns to Luke.

"Did you just hear that? Mum says she taught Joe Huckle from Indigo Joe when he was a child!"

Luke pulls a face of disbelief.

Jake turns back around.

They drive through typical London streets, listening to more of the song, Jake singing and Joni listening hard, still taking it all in.

3

I want to drive a new sports car
And wear only designer clothes
Have a gardener, cleaner and cook
And a bank balance that only grows

Although I want so many things
I ask what happiness they really bring

All I really want is total peace within
And walk within the light
Been looking for it all my life
Been looking for it all my life
Been looking for it all my life
I've searched and searched, oh, yes…

They pull up outside their school, busy with crowds of secondary school age
Joni turns off the engine and shakes her head.

"Let me see that picture again."

Jake shows Joni his phone.

"That's definitely him."

"His brother is in the band too," Jake states.

Joni points to the phone.

"Oh, yes. Noah."

Jake pulls an expression of shock.

"What? He is called Noah," he shouts in further shock.

Luke sits up and leans over them.

"Did you teach him too?"

"No. Just Joe," she smiles.

Jake shakes his head, taking it all in.

"I can't believe you taught him," Jake says to express his shock. He then looks di
up to Joni. "Mind, they're a London based band, and you taught here in London."

Joni smiles at Jake with wide eyes.

"I'm going to tell all my friends about this," Jake announces.

"You'd better run, boys. Have a good day."

Joni remains deep in thought as she watches them walk off together. They turn bac
wave at Joni and then walk on. Joni remains still, staring ahead. She puts her hand
her face with astonishment, shaking her head in disbelief at the turn of the day's eve

TWO

Joni runs back into her house. She shuts the front door, quickly taking off her coat and shoes. She heads into her spare room and straight to a cupboard. She opens the cupboard door to see many boxes. She then pulls out one of the boxes.

She sits down on the floor, opens the box and pulls out many things. She stops when she sees a black book with 'Academic Diary 2001/2002' written on the front.

She flicks through pages that are full of writing. She then closes it and smiles.

"Jonah Huckle," she nostalgically says aloud to herself.

Joni turns to the diary page headed: 'Saturday 1st September 2001', and she avidly reads, reliving her memories.

2001

A younger Joni, now in her twenties with longer and curlier hair, enters the front door of her flat. It is in a hallway with several front doors.

A lady in her late sixties walks by Joni to the next entrance. She is bubbly and friendly in disposition. She is average height with short, curly, grey hair. They look at each other.

"Hi. I've just moved in. I guess you're my neighbour," the lady says to Joni.

"Hi. I am. I live here. I've been here a few years now," Joni replies.

Joni gives her a friendly smile and extends her hand. The lady shakes it with a warm smile and full eye contact.

"I'm Joni."

"I'm Shirley."

"Is it just yourself that's moved in?" Joni asks.

"Just me," Shirley informs her. "How about yourself?"

"Just me too."

Shirley smiles at her and Joni smiles back.

"Did you say Joni? As in the famous singer, Joni Mitchell?"

Joni lets out a laugh as though she's been asked this many times before.

"Yes. My parents were enormous fans of her."

Shirley beams with enthusiasm for this, taking Joni by surprise.

"Me too. An exceptionally talented artist. Have you heard her songs?"

"I did all the time as a child but not these days."

They pause and smile at each other.

"I guess that you work. What do you do?"

"I teach. Six- to seven-year-olds."

Shirley again looks at her with enthusiasm.

"Me too, for my sins," she excitedly tells her.

"Wow! You're a teacher too," Joni confirms.

"Well, I used to be. I'm retired now. I spent forty years of my life as a primary school teacher. I can tell a few stories."

"I bet you can. I've only taught for four years, and I can tell a few!" Joni exclaims.

Shirley studies her.

"You should write it all down. I always wished I had. My only regret is not keeping a diary. I'd love to read forty years of diaries now."

"That's not a bad idea."

Shirley smiles at her.

"Knock any time for a cup of tea."

"And you," Joni returns to her.

"I will do that," Shirley assertively states.

Now inside her flat, Joni is by herself. It is minimalist and tidy. She has a pool table in the living room, taking up a large amount of the area. She picks up her cue and sets the balls into a triangular shape on the table. She takes the first shot to break the triangle of balls, potting two of the balls down from this. One by one, she then pots the other balls.

She then walks to the window. It has a fantastic view of London. She looks out onto the view with a look of gratitude. She is then startled by a knock at the door.

Joni opens her front door, with her pool cue still in her hand. Shirley stands there, holding a large, unused diary. It is black with 'Academic Diary 2001/2002' written on the front. She passes it to Joni.

"I can't stop but have this. I still get given these by a friend but I'm not using it. Start that diary today."

Joni takes it and smiles fondly to her, touched by her thought.

"Thank you. I will."

Shirley looks inquisitively at the pool cue.

"You have a snooker table?"

"A pool table. It's smaller," Joni replies.

Shirley looks genuinely surprised.

"How on Earth did you get it all the way up here?" she asks with amusement.

"With difficulty," Joni laughs; Shirley laughs with her.

"Anyway, I must dash," Shirley says as she walks off.

Now evening, Joni is in her pyjamas and dressing gown. She walks to the window to look at the nighttime view of an illuminated London. She then closes the curtains.

She sees the diary on the side. She smiles on seeing it and picks it up. She then takes a pen from a bag, walks over to her sofa, sits down, opens the diary and starts to write.

2021

Joni remains in her spare room, sat on the floor, engrossed in reading her diary. She looks up and beams at reminiscing on her memories. She closes her diary with a thoughtful expression. She then takes out her phone and calls Stacey. He answers.

"Stacey, are you free to talk?"

"Always. Are you okay?"

"You're never going to believe this. Jake played a song in the car today by a band called Indigo Joe."

"What?"

"No joke. It's Jonah Huckle's band. He's the singer, the front man."

"Jonah? The Jonah Huckle in your class all those years ago?"

"The exact same. Jake showed me his picture."

Stacey pauses and makes a sound to show his surprise.

"I can't believe it. I'm in total shock," Joni breaks the silence.

"You really think it's him?" Stacey questions.

"Oh, Stacey, it's him."

"Wow. You've taken me by surprise. I want to see this picture tonight."

"You can see him now. Just 'Google' him."

"I will," Stacey states. "What a turn up. But what's stranger still is it's the twentieth anniversary of 9/11 tomorrow!" Stacey exclaims.

"His possible prediction of this," Joni shakes her head in shock as she speaks.

"We'll talk on this tonight," Stacey tells her. "But great to hear what he's achieved."

Joni stares ahead and smiles with pleasant surprise.

Still in her spare room, Joni types into her phone to again play 'All My Life'. She listens to the song, emotion overcoming her.

Travelled the world in my quest
Tried to do what I feel best
In many ways I have been blessed
But in other ways so much less…

She then looks down again to the diary. Joni turns to the diary page headed: 'Sunday 2nd September 2001', and she drifts back.

2001

Joni is comfortably sat on the sofa in Shirley's living room. Shirley walks over and puts down a cup of tea next to her. She then sits in a chair opposite.

Joni waits until she has Shirley's attention.

"I started the diary. I've listened to your suggestion, and I'm going to write it all down. It will be interesting to look back on."

Shirley smiles at Joni with a face to show she is pleased to hear this.

"It will be. You won't regret it." Shirley pauses and studies her.

"I bet the children love you," she tells Joni.

Joni smiles shyly at the compliment.

"I love teaching them," Joni beams. "I'm lucky to have the job I do. It's a privilege."

Shirley looks directly at Joni.

"What do they teach you?"

Joni's pulls a face to show she is unsure what she means.

"Has a child ever taught you anything?"

Joni shakes her head.

"What do you mean?"

Shirley smiles at her; Joni looks baffled. They hold their gaze.

"When are you back?" Shirley asks to change the subject and lighten the conversation again.

"Tomorrow! For training though. The kids are back on Thursday."

"And here begins a new school year. Any interesting characters?"

"There's just one," Joni answers. "He's called Jonah." She pauses with a look of intrigue. Shirley nods with interest.

THREE

Joni remains on the floor in her spare room, absorbed in her diary, still listening to 'All My Life' by Indigo Joe.

> _I want to see the wonders of the world_
> _And sail on all its seven seas_
> _Enjoy many good nights out_
> _And be able to do whatever I please_
>
> _I want to lie on a warm, sunny beach_
> _And fly through mountain filled skies_
> _Eat from the finest restaurants_
> _And have all original vinyl I can buy_
>
> _Although I want so many things_
> _I ask what happiness they really bring_
>
> _All I really want is total peace within_
> _And walk within the light_
> _Been looking for it all my life_
> _Been looking for it all my life_
> _Been looking for it all my life_
> _I've searched and searched, oh, yes…_

She turns to the diary page headed: 'Monday 3rd September 2001' and smiles sentimentally to look back.

_2001_

Joni rushes into her school staffroom. It is full and lively. She wades through a crowd, saying hello to some. She sees a spare chair on the end of a row and sits down there. The woman next to her turns around.

"Hi, Joni. Good holiday?"

"Yes, thanks. Yourself?"

"Very good."

Joni, although not a fan of such small talk, politely listens to all she had done over the holiday.

She had attempted to avoid it with the timing of her entrance, but she was now sat with Tracy who was not the most popular among the staff. She always had an opinion, usually that opposed others, and always ensured she voiced it.

Tracy is interrupted by the entrance of Jim Morris, the headteacher. People begin to quieten down to see him. He walks with a stick from a recent knee replacement although maintains a youthfulness most men his age would be envious of. He is in his sixties and close to retirement. He rules the school in a firm but fair manner, being highly respected by his staff, pupils and parents.

He heads to the front of the room. Everyone is now quiet, facing his direction.

"A warm welcome back to everyone. I hope you all had a lovely..."

Jim is interrupted by the school's secretary who is waving at him from the back of the room. He pauses and everyone turns to look towards her. She gestures for him to come with her.

"Talk among yourselves," he addresses his audience. "I'll be back in one moment."

Tracy nods in Jim's direction.

"Oh, I meant to say, Jim wants to see you regarding Jonah," she whispers. "He asked me to mention it if I saw you."

Joni pulls a blank expression.

"Thanks. I will."

"Catch me later too and I'll fill you in on a few things from last year."

Joni nods with intrigue.

Jim returns to the room and everyone, again, faces his direction.

Later in the day, Joni knocks on the door of the Jim's office, standing at the entrance.

He looks up, greeting her with a welcoming smile.

"I hear you wanted to see me."

Jim gets up, pulls out a chair and gestures for her to come in. She walks in and he closes the door behind her.

"Thanks for coming, Joni. Take a seat."

Joni sits down and looks towards him.

"I just wanted to touch base on Jonah."

Joni nods attentively.

"I'm speaking in confidence now. I have some concerns and ask you to come to me on anything, however small."

Joni frowns with a mix of worry and frustration to not have more information.

Jim looks at her to respond.

"Okay."

Jim looks directly at her with an expression to show the importance of what he has to say.

"His behaviour suggests he's possibly on the autistic spectrum, as well as possibly hyperactive." He pauses, deep in thought. "But the Paediatrician's report says he's not either of these."

Joni nods to show she is listening.

"I'm not sure how happy he is at home and that's why I ask you to come to me on anything."

Joni nods again.

"He had a terrible year last year. I'm hoping for improvement. If anyone can get through to him, you can. I believe he needs to feel understood."

"I'll try," she replies in a heartfelt tone.

"I have faith in you. The magic-like way you calm your class may be all he needs."

Joni smiles affectionately at the compliment.

"I hope so."

Jim returns the smile. His expression then swiftly changes to show he has remembered something important.

"Oh, do you remember you've a course next week? The one we discussed last term."

"Yes, I remember. Not the best timing at the beginning of term but it's in my diary."

Jim laughs as he remembers something else.

"Also, we need to place a student in a lower year group for just half a day next week. Can we use you?"

"Yes, of course."

"Thanks, Joni."

Joni smiles at Jim with a look of respect. He reciprocates, showing his respect for her.

Joni walks into Tracy's classroom to see her putting up a wall display.

Tracy catches sight of her and pauses.

"Hi. Did you see Jim?"

"Yes. Just now."

"Did he chat about Jonah?"

"Yes. He did."

"Did he mention that mum had black eyes at the end of last term?"

Joni pulls a face of concern.

"No. He didn't."

Tracy frowns.

"Don't let on that I said, but I think you need to know what you're looking out for."

Joni nods with a blank expression.

"Okay. Thanks." She pauses to think but then decides to ask. "How was Jonah?"

"Difficult. Exhausting."

Joni looks at her to continue.

"Being honest, I didn't get through to him or connect with him. He didn't do any work or read a word all year."

"None?"

Tracy shakes her head.

"His mum says he reads novels at home. She is odd. Very odd. She's into the weird and wonderful. She fills his head with believing he is special in some way which doesn't help him at all."

Joni shows surprise to this.

"It's going to be interesting," she jovially replies but without offering any opinion of her own.

"He's the oldest in the class," Tracy continues. "He has a September birthday. I always thought he should have been kept back a year."

Tracy walks towards the door to leave her room. Joni realises and follows her. Tracy then stops and turns back to Joni.

"One thing. I'm sure you won't, but don't try to hug him. He'll scream."

Joni frowns with intrigue.

"I'd never just try to hug any child."

Back in her classroom, Joni looks through notes on the children in her new class. She gets to Jonah's file. It is thicker than the rest by far. She flicks through, reading bits with interest.

She then puts it down and stares straight ahead with an expression that is a mix of concern and interest.

FOUR

Joni remains in her spare room. She stares ahead with an enormous smile as she listens to the end of 'All My Life' by Indigo Joe.

> *I've been told that life's a test*
> *And of many ways to avoid its mess*
> *I'm working it out for myself I guess*
> *Listening here and there but I dismiss the rest*
> *Because I know I'll find my peace within*
> *And walk within the light*
> *All my life, all my life, all my life, all my life.*

Joni's attention returns to her diary, and she turns to the diary page headed: 'Tuesday 4th September 2001'.

2001

Joni awaits in her classroom; she is sat at her desk and staring ahead. The children are all crowded around the outside door, ready for her to open it and the new school year to begin. She can hear the nerves and excitement in their voices for the day ahead.

She looks up at the clock on the wall, to see it is time to begin.

"Here we go," she says to herself and rises, heading to the door. The children cheer to see her at the door.

She opens it and steps back for the first few to rush in. The rest trickle through in a steady stream. They represent a diverse culture, being from various ethnic backgrounds. They all put their coats away and Joni directs them to sit in the middle of the classroom. This area is free of desks, and she refers to it as the 'carpet area'.

Mrs Morton, Joni's teaching assistant, bounds into the room and the children greet her warmly, showing clearly having worked with her before and to know her well. She is well into her fifties and has many grandchildren, a natural with children.

Joni smiles to see the reception she has received.

Jonah enters. Without putting away his bag or taking off his coat, he sits down on a chair by the window, watching his mother walk into the distance. He is noticeably taller than the others, looking older than six, and has longer hair than the other boys.

Joni watches him, choosing not to intervene.

Mrs Morton sees Jonah and walks over to sit next to him. He moves away a little. She stays put and remains silent.

Joni is now on a chair at the front of the class and the children are all sat around her on the carpet area. Joni addresses the class in a calm, kind and warm manner.

"Well done everyone for coming in so nicely. I hope you all had a lovely summer. My name is Miss Nicholls and I'm your teacher this year."

The children beam at her.

They are interrupted by Mrs Morton.

"Come on, Jonah. Let's join the others in the class."

"No!" he states clearly.

Joni gestures to Mrs Morton to leave him and to come over to the other children. She addresses them to introduce her.

"This is Mrs Morton. She will also work with us."

The children beam again.

Ethan puts up his hand.

Joni nods at him to answer.

"Jonah always does that, Miss," he says to helpfully explain.

"He'll join us when he's ready, Ethan. It's not easy on the first day back."

Chloe puts up her hand.

Joni nods at her to answer.

"What does it say on your badge?"

Joni holds up a lanyard with her name across it.

"This is my name badge, Chloe. It says my name, Miss Nicholls."

"But there are three names on it," Chloe persists. "The middle one looks like Jonah. Are you called Jonah too?"

Joni smiles with endearment.

"No. It says Miss Joni Nicholls. That's my full name but it's Miss Nicholls, in class."

"So, is Joni your real name?" Chloe adds.

"Joni is my first name. Just like your first name is Chloe."

Chloe giggles, content with the answer.

Jonah remains seated and continues to look out of the window. He shows no reaction to his name having been discussed.

The children are now working at their tables, except Jonah who remains by the window, still wearing his coat.

Jim opens the door and peers his head around.

Joni walks over towards him.

"How's everything?" he asks with interest

"The class have made a great start."

Jim smiles and nods towards Jonah.

"Jonah has sat there without saying a word all morning, from the moment he came in," she whispers.

Jim pulls a face to show he is happy.

"Well done."

Joni decides it is time to sit down by Jonah, so she walks around the room but stopping by him and slowly lowering herself. He remains silent, totally ignoring her to begin with. He then glances up at her and they catch each other's eye contact. Joni smiles at him and Jonah smiles back.

"I'm not working!" he declares.

"I can see," Joni jovially replies.

"I'm not writing. I don't want to."

Joni pauses and catches his eye contact.

"Why don't you want to write?" she calmly asks.

He stares at her, a little shocked by her response.

"I will write when I can do it properly. I never do anything until I can do it properly."

"It's okay to make mistakes," Joni tells him. "That's how we all learn."

Jonah glares straight at her and rolls his eyes. He then looks away. Joni continues to attempt to make eye contact but Jonah stares ahead. She realises such answers will switch him off and the questioning approach worked better.

"What can you do properly?"

Jonah looks up again.

"Draw."

Joni smiles to have caught his attention again.

"How about this afternoon you draw the work instead of writing it?"

Jonah shrugs his shoulders.

Chloe comes over to them.

"Hi, Chloe," she welcomes her.

"I like that you are kind to Jonah," she states. "Some teachers get cross."

Later, the children are all working in their places. Joni walks around the room to look at their work, a mix of writing and drawings typical of six-year-olds.

Ben holds up a picture to Joni as she passes him; it looks a little like a monster.

"Do you like mine?"

"Oh, Ben. Yes, I do. Is it a monster?

Ben starts to laugh.

"No. It's you!"

Joni giggles in amusement.

"Oh, yes. It's great. Thanks, Ben."

Loud laughter comes from the book corner. Jonah is there, laughing uncontrollably.

"A monster," he chuckles, barely audible through the hysterics.

Joni and the class all look over to him. He is sat on cushions with paper and a pencil in his hand, leaning on a book, covering his work. He stops laughing to continue to work avidly under this cover.

Joni walks over to him.

"How's yours coming along, Jonah?"

"It's nearly finished."

"Okay. I look forward to seeing it."

Joni walks away with her back turned for only a few seconds.

Jonah shouts after her.

"Miss, I've finished."

Joni turns around, beaming with happiness for his interaction.

Jonah turns the paper over to show her a picture to the standard of someone at an art college. She looks at him, eyes wide and speechless. She then moves closer, and he passes the picture to her. She takes it, her mouth open in astonishment.

Mrs Morton and some children look over to see it, and gasp.

"This is amazing, Jonah," she directly says with surprise. "May I keep it?"

Jonah nods in agreement with an expression that shows he is proud of himself.

"Communication through illustration," he states.

Slightly perplexed, Joni studies him with interest.

FIVE

It is now the end of the first day. The children are sat on the carpet area and Joni heads to the door where their parents await to collect them. She smiles to herself as she walks, happy with the first day of her new class.

She opens the door and, as parents state the name of their child, Joni relays it to the class for them to leave. One by one, the children stand on hearing their name and leave to greet their parent.

With only a few children remaining, including Jonah, Joni steps out to the playground to see a lady rushing towards her room.

"Hi. I'm Steph, Jonah's mum," she announces as she gets near to Joni. She is friendly and full of life. She has a hippie-like appearance with long hair, a flowing skirt and lots of jewellery.

She extends her hand to shake with Joni.

Joni shakes it and smiles to greet her.

"How's he been today?"

Jonah runs over, happy to see her. She hugs him affectionately.

Joni smiles to see him the happiest he has been all day.

"In the morning, he was quiet and withdrawn, sitting by the window and not participating at all."

Jonah pulls a face of annoyance to hear her say this.

"I drew a picture," he indignantly states.

Steph pauses in genuine surprise to hear this.

"But in the afternoon, he drew a picture," Joni jovially adds.

"He drew a picture?" Steph interjects.

"Well, not just a picture. A true work of art! He is an exceptionally talented artist."

Steph looks at him with her mouth open.

He giggles happily to see her expression.

"Jonah, get your picture from my desk to show to your mum," Joni instructs him.

Jonah runs to her desk, gets the picture and runs back to hand it to Steph. She looks at it, and her expression changes to an enormous smile.

"Oh, Jonah, I am so proud of you, and so pleased that you have drawn like this in school."

She turns to Joni.

"He draws like this all the time at home."

"He does?"

"Yes. He won't let me bring them in to show anyone though. He's a talented boy. School hasn't been the right environment for him, but I dreamed of this day."

Joni pauses to take in the moment of Steph's eyes reflecting her happiness.

Jonah tugs Steph's arm.

"Her name is Joni. Joni and Jonah."

Steph's expression shows an interest for her name.

"A lovely name. I'm a big fan of Joni Mitchell. Are you?"

"My parents were fans, so I heard her songs as I was growing up. But I've not played her music for a long while now."

"You need to listen again."

Joni giggles in amusement that her name causes such reactions.

"I have them all on old vinyl from my parents but no record player."

The last couple of parents simultaneously appear to collect their children. Joni nods to acknowledge each of them, and then to the children to inform them.

"She has angels all around her," Jonah tells his mum.

Steph is nonplussed at this and turns to Joni to provide further information.

"He is blessed. He can see angels. I wish I had his gift."

One parent overhears and looks at her with surprise.

Steph sees this and changes the subject.

"Oh, I meant to ask, are you okay with his lunch? He's a fussy eater."

"No one mentioned it, so I guess so," Joni answers.

"Great. Anyway, I must run. The boys have a music lesson on a Tuesday night."

Joni smiles at them, with kindness in her eyes.

Jonah picks up on this and smiles back, holding eye contact.

Joni beams at him to have made a connection.

Joni is now with Jim. They are both at his desk with Jonah's drawing in front of them.

"No," Jim states, unconvinced.

"He started with a blank piece of paper. I am totally certain," Joni insists.

"But you didn't see him draw this?"

"He covered it the whole time he was drawing, but he was drawing."

"Maybe he had it in his bag or found it somewhere," Jim sceptically persists. "He's having you on."

Joni sighs in annoyance.

Jim shakes his head, amused with the situation.

"Get him to draw again and watch him this time."

Now after school, Joni is surrounded by books, marking, in her empty classroom.

Tracy walks in.

"I hear Jonah drew a picture."

Joni holds it up for her to see.

Tracy looks at it and laughs.

"You're winding me up."

Joni shakes her head.

"I think there's more to him than people realise. Did he ever show a sign of being a gifted artist?"

"Err, no," Tracy laughs.

Joni is now in Shirley's living room. They are both on her sofa with cups in their hands.

"A very interesting little boy," Shirley states.

"I need to get him to draw again. I just hope he complies."

Joni pauses, deep in thought.

Shirley pauses to think as well.

"See if he can draw real life objects or people to the same standard," Shirley suggests. "Set a challenge to him. That may be what he needs."

Joni nods with a thoughtful look.

2021

Joni stands up and leaves her spare room with the box still on the floor. She walks down to the kitchen and makes herself a hot drink. She checks her phone to see a missed call from Stacey and a voicemail message.

She opens the message to hear Stacey's voice.

"Joni, I've just googled him. It's him. Definitely! How are you feeling about this? I know you had wondered after him at times, and now this. I'm mind blown!"

"I'm mind blown too," she says to herself.

She finishes making her drink and returns to the spare room, cup in hand. She picks up her diary again, walks to the window, putting down her drink on the windowsill and turns to the page headed: 'Wednesday 5th September 2001'.

_2001_

In Joni's classroom, the children are working at their desks.

Jonah is sat in the book corner but gets up and sits in his place for the first time. At the desk, he stares into space instead of working but Joni cheers inside at this progress. She looks to Mrs Morton who is also elated.

"Well done, Jonah," Mrs Morton encourages.

The children look around and smile at Jonah to see this.

Ethan, on the other hand, scowls at him.

"It's not fair that Jonah doesn't have to work," he announces.

Joni looks at him calmly.

"He's learning to Ethan. He will."

Ethan makes a face at Jonah.

Jonah stares back, annoyed, but then picks up a pencil and almost starts to draw but doesn't. He goes to several times but stops each time.

Joni stares at him, thoughtfully.

Joni and Mrs Morton are alone in the classroom. Joni passes a shell, a plant and a wooden figurine to Mrs Morton.

"Whilst we are all in the hall for PE, could you keep Kali for reading and keep Jonah to do some drawing? Get him to draw these."

"Oh, yes," she beams. "I'd love to see if he really can draw."

"Let's see what he can do."

Mrs Morton nods.

"I'm very intrigued," she tells Joni thoughtfully.

"Me too," Joni replies. "I'm also very intrigued."

SIX

In the school hall, the children are in their PE lesson, led by Joni. They are in individual spaces, listening to Joni and copying her stretches.

Mrs Morton comes in with Kali and Jonah.

"Kali did some fantastic reading but now really wants to do PE," Mrs Morton states.

Joni nods.

"Kali, well done."

Mrs Morton pauses to catch Joni's attention with a large grin.

"Jonah has sat and drawn the whole time," Mrs Morton excitedly announces. "Miss Nicholls, you must see these pictures."

Mrs Morton holds up the pictures, again to a professional standard.

Joni beams in delight to Jonah.

"Jonah, these are brilliant," she tells him as her eyes light up. "Can you take these straight to Mr Morris?"

The children look over with impressed expressions.

"Mr Morris, the Head?" Jonah frowns, shaking his head.

Joni nods her head, confused.

"No. I can't show Mr Morris."

"Why not?"

"I don't think he will want to see me. He thinks I'm naughty."

"He does think he's naughty," Kali informs Joni.

"Then go and show him how talented you are. He 'will' want to see you."

Mrs Morton takes the pictures from Joni.

"Come on, Jonah."

Jonah reluctantly follows Mrs Morton.

Back in the classroom, Joni reads a story to the children.

Jonah bursts in, full of pride. The children turn around to look at him. He shows them all a 'Head Award' sticker.

"He 'did' like them," Jonah declares, unable to contain himself with emotion.

The children clap for him, with big smiles.

Jonah beams as he watches, a little overwhelmed. His eyes turn to Joni, and he gives her the biggest, heart-warming smile.

"I knew he would. Well done, Jonah," Joni tells him, returning the smile. Her eyes reflecting it is these moments that make the job so rewarding to her.

Jonah walks over to her to catch her attention.

"Communication through illustration," he boldly replies.

"What do you mean by that, Jonah?" she questions.

He looks at her, shocked she doesn't know.

"It's when words are not necessary."

Joni nods, thinking about the phrase.

It is the end of the school day, and the children are sat on the carpet area with their coats on, ready to leave, whilst Joni is on a chair at the front.

Zain puts his hand up.

Joni nods to answer.

"Can we play the 'Ask the teacher' game?" he asks.

Joni looks puzzled.

"What's that?"

"We ask you questions, and you answer them."

"Oh, Zain. I don't know," Joni stutters.

"I'll start," he shouts. "How much money do you have?"

Joni laughs with amusement.

"I don't have any money. Sorry."

Connor puts up his hand.

Joni nods to answer.

"Why don't you have a tummy?"

Joni looks directly at him with confusion.

"Connor, of course I have a tummy."

"But it is so small and skinny," he states. "Not like Mrs Morton. She has a big tummy."

Joni pauses in genuine shock and looks over apologetically to Mrs Morton.

Mrs Morton laughs it off and gestures that it doesn't matter.

"I think we'll leave 'Ask the teacher' for today," Joni informs the class.

Jonah shows no sign of engagement and appears totally switched off.

Most children have now left, and the same few are left as were before.

Steph bursts into the room; Jonah's brother is with her.

"I heard you have a 'Head Award', Jonah," she states, ecstatic.

Jonah jumps up with excitement and gives his mum a hug, smiling ear to ear.

She hugs him tightly back and kisses the top of his head.

"I'm so, so proud of you."

Steph turns to Joni with genuine gratitude.

"You've no idea what this means. Sincerely, thank you."

"They are Jonah's drawings," Joni smiles in reply.

"But he's comfortable enough to do them. This has never happened before. He's been quite a problem here in the past. This means everything."

Joni smiles warmly at her.

Steph nods towards Noah.

"This is Noah, Jonah's big brother."

Noah smiles at Joni and she smiles back at him.

"I named both of my children when I was going through a Christian phase and was particularly interested in aquatic hero stories in the Bible," Steph announces.

Joni looks bemused but smiles.

Two parents overhear and give a look to each other to suggest she is strange.

Joni notices and smiles at them, forcing them to change their expressions.

Joni is back in Shirley's living room. Shirley shakes her head with intrigue.

"She sounds quite a unique lady."

Joni smiles to herself, distantly deep in thought.

Shirley frowns with intrigue, realising there is more to her expression.

"Are you okay?"

Joni thinks about her answer before she speaks.

"I can't put my finger on it but there's something about her that reminds me of my mum."

Joni looks down, deep in thought, with an expression of pain.

Shirley smiles at her, in empathy.

"I'll make another tea," she tells Joni in a calm, caring tone.

2021

Joni puts the diary down and continues to search through the memory box. She pulls out the three pictures drawn by Jonah of the shell, plant and figurine. She smiles to herself and picks up the diary again.

She turns to the page headed: 'Thursday 6th September 2001' with a nostalgic smile.

2001

It's another busy morning with the children entering the classroom. Ben's mum comes in, carrying Ben at arm's length, as he cries. Joni walks over sharply.

"Is he okay?" she asks with concern.

Ben's mum has a jovial look overshadowing her stress.

"He's tripped over and fallen in dog mess. Can I take him somewhere to change him into his PE kit and then take his clothes home to wash?"

"Of course," Joni replies with relief it is nothing more serious.

Mrs Morton comes over and Joni looks at her apologetically.

"Come on, Ben," Mrs Morton says to him kindly, reading Joni's expression.

"Thank you," Joni states sincerely.

The children at the front of the classroom are holding their noses.

"It smells bad in here," Chloe announces.

"The classroom smells of Ben's dog poo," Zain adds.

Some children groan, some laugh and some pulls expressions of disgust.

Jonah turns to Joni.

"They're being unkind. Ben will feel bad."

"I won't let that happen," Joni instantly replies.

Jonah then hands her a ten pence piece.

Joni looks at him quizzically.

"This is for you."

"Me?" she questions kindly.

"You said you didn't have any money."

"Oh, Jonah. I can't take it, but it means so much that you thought of me."

Jonah sits down on the carpet with the others whilst Joni watches him, with endearment.

SEVEN

The children are now sat on the carpet area in front of Joni for a numeracy lesson. They each have an individual whiteboard on their lap and a pen in their hand. On the main board, are a list of sums that require adding two 2-digit numbers together. Joni points to the first on the list.

"Can you all try this one on your whiteboards?" she asks them.

The children attempt this and work together.

Jonah's board is empty. He stares at the front of the class with no engagement.

"Can you write numbers? Not words, but numbers?" Joni whispers to him.

Jonah shrugs his shoulders but then covers his board and starts to write on it. He writes with increased speed. He then puts his board face down so no one can see it.

"Everyone to their places to start on today's work," Joni instructs them.

The children go to their places, except Jonah. Once out of sight of another child, he holds up his board for just Joni to see it. It has a list of sums with the answers.

Joni looks at him and smiles in delight.

"That's all of today's work, all correct."

Jonah looks at her, happy with himself.

Joni walks into Jim's office and holds up the whiteboard of additions.

"Jonah did this in seconds. It's all the work that was on the board."

Jim studies it, checking the answers, and then up at Joni, shaking his head in amazement.

"What a fantastic start to the year. Very well done."

Joni smiles.

"Anything concerning?" Jim adds.

"No. Mum is eccentric but loving and caring."

Jim pauses but then decides to ask.

"Does she seem okay?"

Joni looks at him before answering.

"Yes. She was so happy with the sticker you gave him."

Jim smiles.

"Why are you worried?" Joni asks out of concern.

"Have you met dad?"

Joni shakes her head, but Jim says nothing further.

"The dad is your concern?" Joni asks.

Jim doesn't reply but his lack of response tells Joni all she needs to know.

"I'll keep an eye out," she informs him.

In her classroom, Joni stands by the window and watches the children play. She sees Jonah walking around by himself, so she goes to the door and opens it.

"Jonah," she shouts out to him.

Jonah walks straight over to Joni.

"How about we see if there are a couple of children from the class that you can draw?" she asks in a calm tone.

"Their whole body or just their face?" he asks blankly.

"I was thinking just their face."

"Okay," he states, and skips off.

Joni watches him go. She continues to watch him play alone with a sadness washing over her.

The children come into the classroom from break, and Jonah walks over to Joni.

"Miss, Kai says I can draw him."

Joni smiles.

"How about we do it tomorrow at break time?"

Jonah nods his head enthusiastically, beaming at her.

"We could get another friend as well?" she asks him.

He again enthusiastically nods his head.

"I can't wait for this," he states.

Joni gives him an enormous smile to hear this.

The children are in their places, working hard, whilst Joni walks around the room.

Jonah is in his seat and draws another detailed picture to a very high standard instead of conducting any written work. He is totally absorbed and no longer covers his work.

Jim puts his head around the door. He looks at Jonah and then at Joni. He pulls a face to Joni to show he is very impressed to see this.

It is lunch break, and the children are outside whilst Joni is in her classroom alone, tidying around. Mrs Morton comes in, startling her.

"Hi Joni. You need to know; Jonah has been hysterical in the lunch hall."

Joni pauses from tidying with a look of concern.

"Hysterical?"

Mrs Morton nods.

"What happened?"

Mrs Morton walks into the room and sits down before answering.

Joni stares, waiting to hear.

"A piece of cling film touched him. It was the child next to him. No harm was meant. Turns out he has a phobia of cling film, thinking it will suffocate him."

Joni nods with understanding and sadness.

"He's been taken out and is calming down," Mrs Morton continues.

The children begin entering the classroom, coming in from their lunchtime. They immediately sit down on the carpet area.

Jonah also enters and joins them on the carpet but begins to fidget about.

Joni gestures for Mrs Morton to sit with him.

She goes over to him, but he lies down on the floor.

"Come on Jonah, shall we sit up ready for Miss Nicholls?"

Jonah stays on the floor, staring up at the ceiling. He then suddenly starts to roll and thrash himself about, laughing at his own disobedience.

Ethan turns to Joni with a face of disappointment.

"This is what he used to be like, Miss."

The children look at him to suggest they think he is odd, moving away from him. There is a growing space around him with the other children scrunched up towards the edges of the carpet area. Jonah thrashes himself harder, making use of the increased space.

Joni looks at him to catch eye contact.

Jonah notices and stares back at her. He then calms down and sits up.

Joni looks surprised that he complied so willingly.

"Can we all move back into the space?" she addresses the children.

Caleb throws an expression of annoyance to Jonah.

"We're avoiding Jonah because he may go really crazy."

Joni nods to Caleb to accept his point of view.

"You may also want to avoid bullets and darts," Jonah shouts whilst laughing loudly at himself.

Some children laugh and others look at him perplexed.

Jonah then sits bolt upright and puts his hand up.

Joni nods for him to answer.

"I need the toilet."

"You may go but can you be quick?" she sighs, unsure if letting him go will be the correct decision.

"I drank a lot of water at lunchtime so I'm not sure I can be quick," he laughs. "It may be a long one."

Jonah laughs to himself as he leaves. Some children laugh and others just stare at him.

Joni gestures to Mrs Morton to follow him. She gets up to walk out and heads to the door.

Jonah then bursts back in with a thick, black marker pen in his hand. He has drawn a beard and moustache on his face with it. The children laugh.

"Someone has left a black pen out there," he announces, finding himself hilarious.

Joni and Mrs Morton catch each other's glare. Joni nods to Mrs Morton to go with Jonah.

"I'll keep him outside and get him to wash his face once he's calmer," she tells Joni.

"Thank you," Joni replies with sincerity.

Joni looks back at the class and Ethan has his hand up. She nods at him to speak.

"Miss," he hesitates.

"Yes, Ethan."

"Lewis has put a snake on your foot."

Joni looks down and there is a plastic snake on her foot.

She screams in surprise and kicks it off to the side, a moment of letting her guard down.

Lewis smiles cheekily at her as she then composes herself and picks it up. Some of the children scream on seeing the plastic snake.

She then puts it on her desk and shakes her head in bemusement.

The children begin to laugh, and, on this occasion, Joni cannot contain her own amusement, laughing with them.

She looks around the classroom at the children laughing and smiles to herself, knowing it is the moments such as these that are special.

EIGHT

At home time, Jonah has not yet returned to the classroom. Steph has arrived and Joni shows her the whiteboard with his additions on.

Steph absolutely beams, shaking her head with astonishment.

"I'm just so pleased to see he's worked in maths. I thought this would be the least likely lesson he would work in. I must confess I've never done any maths with the boys. I'm too creative."

Joni smiles as she speaks but her expression changes to a look of seriousness.

"Unfortunately, his behaviour declined this afternoon. During lunch, he was touched by a piece of cling film."

Steph looks saddened to hear this.

"Oh, no. He's petrified of cling film touching him. Has he played up since?"

Joni nods.

"He lost his focus. He was disruptive and then drew a beard and moustache on his own face. He has spent the afternoon outside of the classroom with Mrs Morton."

"I'll chat with him. I don't want to go back to where we were last year, especially after this fantastic start."

"Thank you, I also want him to maintain his fantastic start," Joni tells her.

Steph and Joni pause their conversation, but Steph breaks the silence.

"He was suffocated in a past life and that's where this fear comes from."

Another parent gives a look of amusement at her comment.

Mrs Morton enters the classroom with Jonah. Some black pen remains on his face.

"Oh, Jonah. Your face," Steph says quietly, with some disappointment.

Jonah stares at her with a guilty expression as she shakes her head. He then changes to being excited.

"I'm drawing some people in the class tomorrow at break time."

"Only if there is a change in behaviour," Joni states clearly.

"Jonah," Steph says to get his attention. "That's fair."

"Joe!" he declares.

Joni looks startled.

Steph turns to Joni.

"He wants to be known as Joe going forward, instead of Jonah."

Jonah looks at his mum, his eyes pleading for her to give in.

Steph sighs.

"I will always call him Jonah, but maybe he can be known as Joe at school?"

Joni looks at Jonah with a face to suggest it isn't a problem.

"That works for me," she tells him. "So, it's Joe from now on?"

Joe nods happily.

Joni is now with Shirley, in her living room. They are both on the sofa with cups in their hands, deep in conversation.

"Another new one on me," Shirley tells her, with an expression of bemusement. "I never had a parent talk of a previous life."

Joni lets out a small laugh and shakes her head.

"She's totally crazy. But endearing."

Joni looks at the piano in the corner and nods towards it.

"Do you play?" she asks Shirley.

"Oh, yes. I used to be the one who played the piano in assemblies. Oh, I used to so love doing that."

"We use a CD player now."

"Times change. Soon they'll be using computers instead of CD players!" Shirley laughs at the thought.

"Play me a song," she hopefully asks Shirley.

Shirley looks in two minds.

"I don't play that much these days. I tell you what. I'll play, if you sing along."

Joni pulls a face to suggest she'd rather not, but Shirley pulls one back to suggest she won't change her mind.

"Only if you sing too," Joni asks, thinking it a fair compromise.

"You're as stubborn as me," Shirley laughs.

She smiles at Joni but goes to the piano, taking a book from the top of it - a book of old school assembly songs. She flicks through and then passes it to Joni.

"Use the book for the lyrics."

Joni takes it and flicks through.

"These songs remind me of my own school days!" Joni exclaims.

"Do you remember this one?" Shirley asks as she plays some music.

Joni jumps up.

"Autumn Days! We sung that all the time at my primary school."

Shirley laughs but sings the first line.

"Autumn days when the grass is jewelled…"

"I love that song," Joni tells Shirley.

"Me too," Shirley says enthusiastically. "It always reminds me of returning to school after the long summer break. It always suddenly feels like autumn, if you get what I mean?"

"Yes, I do. It's suddenly autumn."

"It certainly is. Shall we sing this one?"

Joni nods, and they both sing Autumn Days together with Shirley playing the piano.

"That was brilliant," Joni states as they finish.

"Nothing beats a good sing song. How about another?" Shirley asks her.

"Go on. Then I had better head back."

"You choose."

Joni flicks through and stops.

"This one. One More Step."

Shirley looks over.

"I know it. You keep the book."

"This reminds me of every new class and the children taking another step forward in life," Joni smiles.

Shirley starts to play, and they both sing together.

"One more step along the world I go…"

"One more," Joni laughs as they finish. "You choose."

"How about The Best Gift?" Shirley suggests.

"Oh, yes. I remember that one too."

"It reminds me of the things that matter in life and all the morals I did my best to teach them."

Joni smiles affectionately at her.

"You said you thought the children would love me. I bet you were an amazing teacher, and they loved you too," Joni tells her.

"I can only hope so."

"I'm so glad you moved in next door," Joni shares, smiling at her.

Shirley smiles affectionately back.

"Me too."

"What made you move to a small flat?" Joni asks her.

"I didn't need my large house after losing my husband, so I sold up and moved here."

"I'm sorry to hear that."

"He was older than me and had been ill for a few years."

Joni smiles with empathy.

"I did the same, after I inherited my parents' house. It was too big for just me, so I sold it and bought here. I love it here. It's perfect."

Shirley smiles at her with empathy.

"Anyway," Joni states to change the subject, "Let's sing, The Best Gift."

"Let's," agrees Shirley.

She begins to play the piano, and they both begin to sing.

"I will bring to you the best gift I can offer…"

Joni claps as they finish, and Shirley joins her.

"I best go. School in the morning," Joni laughs.

"It's nearly the weekend," Shirley adds. "I bet you're exhausted."

"Yes. The first week back is always so tiring."

"I remember it well. One more day of school and then you can relax a little for two days."

"Relax! I'm a teacher. Always work to do. Most of my weekend will involve working."

Shirley pauses to throw her an expression of seriousness.

"You need to relax."

Joni nods to accept defeat.

"This has been relaxing. Fun too. We must do it again."

"Definitely," Shirley smiles warmly to her.

Back in her flat, Joni picks up her pool cue and puts the balls into the triangle. She hits the white ball with her cue to hit the triangle of balls and break them. Two yellow balls fall into holes. She then pots the rest of the yellow balls and the black.

She puts down her cue and smiles to herself. She looks over to a photo of her with her parents on her graduation day. She picks it up to look closer, smiles with a sadness and then puts it down again.

She then begins to get herself ready for bed, singing some of 'The Best Gift' to herself as she does.

NINE

Joni, sat on the floor in her spare room and diary in hand, turns the page to the next date, headed: 'Friday 7th September 2001'.

"Oh, my goodness," she says to herself. "This was a day I've never forgotten."

2001

That morning, Jonah walks into the classroom and sits with the other children. He looks up and smiles to Joni.

"I see we have Joe," Joni announces. "Morning, Joe."

The children look around to see who she is referring to.

"Morning," Joe pipes up, proud to be addressed with the updated version of his name.

"Are you Joe now?" Chloe asks.

"Yes," he boldly replies.

The children are now sat on the carpet area in front of her.

"Today, we're going to all write a poem on a feeling of our choice," Joni informs them with excitement and enthusiasm.

The children sit up, mimicking this enthusiasm with their body language.

"Can anyone tell me a feeling?"

Some children put their hands up.

Joni nods to each in turn to answer.

"Happy," says Kai.

"Excited," adds Ethan.

"Miserable," laughs Ben as he pulls the most unhappy face he can.

The children laugh, finding him amusing.

"Tired," says Chloe sensibly.

"Angry," laughs Lewis, pulling an angry face.

Ben laughs at him.

"Great answers but let's now think about angry," Joni asks them. "We're going to try to describe angry using our five senses. Give me one of the senses."

33

"Touch," answers Kali.

"Good answer," smiles Joni. "Let's think of something we can touch. How does it feel when we're angry?"

Ethan waves his hand ferociously, brimming to spill his idea.

"Like breaking glass."

"Great answer. Angry feels like breaking glass."

Joni writes it on the board.

"Give me another sense."

"Hearing," answers Zain.

"Great. How does it sound when we're angry?"

Milly waves her hand.

"Like cars beeping in traffic jams."

"Great answer, Milly. Angry sounds like cars beeping in a traffic jam."

Joni writes it on the board.

"Class, you are now going to write your own emotion poems, choosing your own emotion and writing for all five senses. What are the other three senses?"

The children are now at work in their places, but Joe has stayed on the carpet area, staring into space.

Ethan gives him a look of irritation.

"It's not fair!" he exclaims. "Jonah's not working again."

"It's Joe now," he shouts back. "And I am working. I'm doing my poem in my head."

The children all stop and look at Jonah sat motionless and speechless. They look confused and then look away to return to their work.

Joni studies him with interest.

The children are back on the carpet area, each holding their work. Ethan stands at the front, speaking to the class confidently.

> *"Excitement feels like worms in your tummy*
> *Excitement sounds like cheering when you score a goal*
> *Excitement looks like candles burning on your birthday cake*
> *Excitement smells like biscuits baking in the oven*
> *Excitement tastes like ice cream and sprinkles"*

The children clap for him, impressed.

"Well done, Ethan. That's a fantastic poem," Joni proudly tells him.

Mrs Morton smiles warmly to congratulate him too.

Ethan sits down on the carpet with the others, beaming to himself.

Joe's hand shoots up.

"Joe, would you like to tell us yours?" Joni asks, a little weary with him having nothing written down.

"Yes," he states clearly. "But mine's a bit longer and I have made it rhyme."

"We'd love to hear it."

Joe stands up without anything to read.

The class looks over with interest, as Mrs Morton and Joni catch each other's eyes.

"I'm doing lonely," he states. "Because I have often felt very lonely."

Mrs Morton and Joni again catch each other's eyes, both hopeful for Joe.

Everyone watches Joe intently as he moves to the front.

He pauses to check the children are all watching him and then reads out his poem from his memory.

"Lonely feels like a dark, grey world
A world that's made of stone
I wish I didn't feel it
I don't want to be alone

Lonely sounds like silence
There is no noise to hear
Except the beating of my heart
That beats so loud with fear

Lonely looks like an empty park
With a swing swaying in the breeze
Could someone here be my friend?
Just one person, please

Lonely smells like burning wood
On a cold bonfire night
The fireworks may look pretty
But they're a fading light

Lonely tastes like cabbage
And all the foods I hate
My mum says I will find some friends
But I don't, I wait and wait"

Joni watches in amazement and with increasing emotion, as does Mrs Morton and the children. Joni and Mrs Morton look to each other with their mouths open.

There is silence for a moment as the children also look on in amazement.

As Joe finishes, Ethan stands up and claps for him. Other children join him and stand to clap. Joni and Mrs Morton join in. The whole class is now in a standing ovation.

As the claps fade, Joni gestures to them to sit again. She stares at Joe, wondering how she can express the level of emotion within her. He has genuinely shocked her.

The class is silent, waiting for Joni to speak.

"Oh, Joe, what an amazing poem," she says slowly and softly. "I'm lost for words. This is one is the best poems I have ever heard."

Mrs Morton looks over to Joni and the class.

"This is a moment I will never forget, ever," she tells them.

"Me neither," Joni adds.

Joni and Mrs Morton lock eyes, smiling to each other.

"I would like to be Joe's friend," Ben tells the class.

"And me," says Chloe.

"And me," say many others, simultaneously.

Joni watches, trying to suppress a tear forming in her eye.

"I think another round of applause for Joe," Joni says.

The class again enthusiastically clap him.

When the clapping dies down, Joni addresses them.

"Joe and Ethan, can you both go with Mrs Morton and, Joe, tell it to her once again for her to write it down."

They both nod.

Joni then gets the attention of Mrs Morton to check she is happy to.

"Certainly," she replies with a smile.

"Then you can take your poems to Mr Morris for a 'Head Award' each."

Joe beams with happiness.

TEN

Joe, Chloe, Ben and Kai are in the classroom whilst the other children are outside at break time. Joe is drawing Ben. This picture is turning into another to a professional standard. Joni looks over and smiles to see him happy.

"Can we play 'Ask the teacher' as it's just us?" Chloe enquires.

Joni looks at her with an expression to say she would rather not.

"We'll let Joe concentrate."

"I can concentrate and play," Joe contests. "I'll start. Do you have a husband?"

"I'm a Miss. Miss Nicholls. You are 'Miss' if you are not married and 'Mrs' if you are."

"If you're not married, who looks after you?" he persists.

Joni smiles kindly at him.

"I look after myself."

Joe looks at her thoughtfully.

"Do you get lonely?"

Joni pauses to think about her answer, feeling it closer to the truth than she would like.

"Oh Joe, I'm an adult. I'm fine."

Joni looks away, thoughtfully.

Joni is now in her classroom, marking books whilst the children are at lunch, when Mrs Morton enters. Her face suggests there has been an incident.

"Joe has been brought inside again," she says sadly. "He's crying uncontrollably."

Joni looks at her directly, genuinely saddened.

"Oh, no. Why?"

"Two boys had a fight on the playground. He wasn't involved but seeing it has upset him."

Joni looks concerned and shakes her head in acknowledgement.

"Can I bring him to see you?" Mrs Morton asks.

"Of course."

Joe comes into the classroom to see Joni. He sits down next to her, head down.

Joni tries to catch his eye contact.

"Hi, Joe. I hear you were upset."

He looks up at her, silently, with sad eyes. He just shrugs his shoulders.

"Were any of the children mean to you?"

He shakes his head.

"What has made you feel so upset?" she asks tentatively.

"They're all mean to each other. I don't like it."

Joni studies him.

"I know it's not nice when children are unkind to each other."

Joe shrugs his shoulders.

"You made friends with Ben, Chloe and Kai earlier. Why not run out and find them? You could tell them you feel sad. You may feel better by talking."

Joe turns to face her.

"I don't want to talk to 'them' about feeling sad," he states assertively. "The person I want to talk to…" Joe tails off. He looks directly at Joni and continues, "…is dead!"

Joni stares at him, taken by surprise. She pauses to gather her thoughts.

"Who do you want to talk to?" she asks him kindly.

"My grandad."

Joni, again, pauses before answering.

"You can still talk to him. Find a quiet place and just tell him all you want to say."

"I do sometimes, but the others think I'm talking to myself and I'm weird."

"Could you do it at home?"

Joe nods his head to dismiss her. He then looks up at Joni with intrigue.

"Miss, do you know about light world?"

Joni shakes her head.

"What is light world?"

Joe stares directly at her, studying her, but whispers to explain.

"I go there every night as a spirit. I'm so happy there. It's white and peaceful, and everyone is so kind to each other. Best of all, my grandad is there too. You will go there too one day. Then it's called a 'Garden of light', but that's when you die."

Joni smiles at him with empathy. Joe looks out of the window and pauses to watch. They hold this silence.

Joe then sees Kai through the window.

"Oh, there's Kai. Can I go out again now?"

Joni nods to answer.

He wastes no time and runs out to him.

Joni goes to the window to watch.

Jonah runs to Kai, but Kai runs straight by him, not noticing him. Joe looks disheartened by this and just stands still with a sad face.

Joni continues to look out of the window with an expression of sadness.

Joni is with Jim, in his office, both clearly in a heavy discussion.

"Children can have very vivid imaginations. I've known other boys invent whole worlds, involving space and such."

Joni shakes her head.

"This was different."

Jim shakes his head to her.

"The world has changed. They play computer games. They watch all sorts on the television. They are surrounded by technology. We worry too much on health and safety to just let them play. The list goes on. It all has an effect. Some are more sensitive and vulnerable than others, such as Jonah."

"Joe," she corrects him. "He's Joe now."

"It's escapism. He's with his grandad again. Mum lost her dad earlier this year, devastating them all. They were all very close."

"No one mentioned that!" Joni adds.

"Did Tracy not?"

"No."

Jim pulls a face.

"But, neither did you," Joni adds.

Jim pulls an expression to show he'll take it on the chin.

"I apologise for that, but I try to not give out such information."

Joni nods to him in acknowledgement.

"What's he escaping from?" she asks.

"His difference, his sensitivity, his inability to make friends, losing his grandad, arguing parents, an eccentric mother, a father that doesn't understand him and the list goes on."

Joni listens but with a distance washing over her face as she goes deep into thought.

Joni flashes back to herself in her late teens, at the funeral of the last of her two parents. She is greatly distressed, and others are around her, comforting her.

Joni remains lost in her thoughts, staring blankly away from Jim.

He looks at her with empathy.

"Are you okay?"

Joni looks back at him and nods.

"Teaching isn't easy. You're doing so well with this little boy. Be proud of what you have achieved."

Joni smiles, slightly shyly at the compliment, and then composes herself.

2021

Joni stares down at the page with an emotional nostalgia in her eyes.

"And these days we add social media in that list, Jim," she says to herself.

She is startled by her phone ringing.

She sees the name 'Stacey' across the screen and answers.

"Joni," he shouts, full of enthusiasm. "It is him!"

Joni laughs.

"I know."

"I did leave a voicemail, but I wanted to call when I had the chance to," Stacey shouts with excitement. "It's him! Without doubt, it is him."

Joni laughs again.

"I've just been looking back through my old diary and reading about him in my class."

"Wow, I bet it's insightful."

"Very. How is it twenty years ago?"

"I know. Twenty years since 9/11."

"Where did that time go?"

"Stacey, I often wonder what the children I taught are like now, what they are doing and hoping they are happy. You never imagine this."

"No, you don't, but Joe was destined for great things."

"It's just so phenomenal to see this. It's taken me back but made my day."

"Joni, we must watch the news coverage of the twentieth anniversary of 9/11."

"Definitely. We'll involve the boys, and I'll tell them the story of Joe around this."

"Joe and 9/11 go hand in hand really, don't they?" Stacey states.

"Well, that's the main reason I never forgot him."

ELEVEN

Joni opens her diary again and flicks through the pages to find where she left off.

"Where was I?" she says to herself.

She finds her page and stops flicking.

"Oh, yes. Still on Friday 7th September 2001."

2001

Joni is sat with Lewis as he reads to her.

"The monkey climbed the tree and swung on the branches," he sounds out slowly.

Joni reads the same book with Milly.

"He saw a stream and stopped to have a drink," she reads, more fluent than Lewis.

Joni then shows the same book to Joe. He looks at it and rolls his eyes. He opens it and reads the pages, speedily and perfectly.

He then closes the book and repeats back all he has just read.

"The monkey climbed the tree and swung on the branches. As he swung, he looked below. He saw a stream and stopped to have a drink," he reads on to repeat the rest of the book, word perfect.

Joni looks at him, mouth open in shock.

He giggles to Joni with the biggest smile.

"Can you remember other books you've read?" she asks him.

"Yes. I have a library in my head."

Joni smiles affectionately at him.

"I can see the pages in my head, and I just read off those," he adds. "My mum says it's a photographic memory. My brain takes a photo of the page, and I can read off it later."

"That's an amazing gift to have. Do you read a lot at home?"

"Yeah. Every night with mum and Noah."

"Do you read with your dad?"

Joe gets up and starts to walk off.

Joni looks shocked and calls back to him.

"Joe, I didn't mean to upset you."

He turns to face her.

"I want to go back now."

Joni nods to allow him.

Joe turns around and walks back.

Joni watches him with an expression of intrigue.

At home time, Joni is in the classroom with Steph, Joe by her side.

"Another 'Head Award'!" she exclaims, giving him a big hug.

"He wrote a fantastic poem."

Steph looks up in surprise.

"He wrote it down?"

"Oh, no," Joni replies. "He read out from memory. We have since written it down."

Joni hands the poem to Steph.

"He has an amazing gift for poetry," Joni informs her. "Well beyond his years."

Steph takes the poem and begins to read it in her head.

"We read and write a lot of poetry at home. This is like one I wrote with the boys on loneliness. But, well remembered Jonah, and very well adapted."

"Joe!" he shouts. "I'm in school and I'm Joe in school!"

Joni turns to Steph.

"Oh, he's remembered it?"

"There are crossovers, but he's adapted it well."

"Still, an amazing achievement," Joni informs them both. "He showed he had a photographic memory when reading today."

"He does. He's very lucky."

Steph pauses and looks at Joni with deep gratitude.

"He's achieved more this week than in the previous three years. I can't say how happy I am."

Joni smiles at her and to Joe.

"Can I play outside?" he asks his mum.

"Yes. I'll only be a moment."

Joni waits until he is out of hearing distance.

"He also mentioned his light world."

Steph looks genuinely surprised.

"He trusts you to tell you that."

Joni smiles.

"That came about after my dad died," she confides. "He meets him there as a spirit. I do believe he's connected to the spirit world."

Joni nods.

"Does your husband believe this also?"

Steph's expression changes.

"He doesn't," she says flatly and pauses. She takes a deep breath. "He blames me for Joe's difficulties at school. He thinks my beliefs have caused Joe's problems. We don't really agree on much at all anymore."

Joni nods empathetically to her in acknowledgement.

2021

Joni, immersed in her diary, turns to the page headed: 'Saturday 8th September 2001'.

2001

Joni and Shirley are in Shirley's living room, on the sofa with cups in their hands.

"Quite a week!" Shirley announces.

Joni nods to agree with an amused expression.

"Thanks for listening."

"Any time," Shirley tells her.

Joni looks thoughtfully to her.

"I feel as though I have a parent again."

Shirley beams to hear this.

"I'll look out for you. As a mother myself, I know your parents would like that."

"You're a mother," Joni asks with some surprise. "You never mentioned it."

Shirley looks down.

Joni looks at her with intrigue.

"You don't have any photos of your family up," Joni dares to state to see if she'll confide.

"I have a cupboard of photos."

"Do you see your son or daughter?"

"I had two daughters but one died in a car accident. Her boyfriend was driving too fast."

Joni looks genuinely saddened, looking at her with empathy.

"I'm so sorry to hear that."

"I'm okay. It was some time ago. I do wonder what she would be doing now if the accident hadn't happened, but I'm at peace."

Joni nods.

"I understand. I miss my parents, but I'm at peace."

Shirley smiles with kindness.

"My other daughter moved to Australia. I've two grandchildren there."

"Wow. Have you visited?"

"Yes. I go every Christmas. We speak on the phone, but I do wish they were nearer. So, only the one daughter, and she's the other side of the world."

"I was an only daughter. It was always the three of us. I miss them so much."

"They would be so proud of you," Shirley tells her. "They wouldn't want you to be alone. They'd like you to meet someone and have your own family."

Joni smiles with how cleverly she put that into the conversation.

"The only time I'm going to meet a man is if one suddenly walks through my classroom."

They both laugh.

"Join a club or go out with a friend?" Shirley suggests.

"Maybe one day. I'm okay on my own."

Joni straightens herself, sitting up to show she means it.

"Think about it. You don't want to spend your weekends alone," Shirley continues.

"I'll think."

Shirley pulls a face, mixed of amusement and exasperation.

2021

Joni, engrossed in her diary, turns to the page headed: 'Sunday 9th September 2001'.

2001

Joni plays pool on the pool table in her flat, potting several balls down including the black ball. She puts the cue down, grabs her coat and heads towards the front door of the flat.

Joni walks along the River Thames and by the Embankment area in London. She pauses by the river, learns over the edge and stares ahead, deep in thought. She hears Shirley's voice saying back to her, "You don't want to spend your weekends alone."

44

TWELVE

2021

Joni, still hooked, turns to the diary page headed: 'Monday 10th September 2001'.

"Twenty whole years ago today," she says to herself, shaking her head. "The day it happened. The day of the premonition. The day I've never forgotten."

2001

It is Monday morning, and the children enter the classroom, following their weekend. They take off their coats and put their bags away.

Steph and Noah come to the classroom entrance. Steph is stressed in her manner. Joe can be heard screaming uncontrollably, sat down in the middle of the playground. Joni looks out to him. Children and parents are looking over in concern.

Joni gestures to Mrs Morton to come to the front of the class and then walks hurriedly over to them.

She looks to Steph for an explanation.

"He's had a terrible dream. He's hardly slept. I can't get him any closer to the classroom."

"What did he dream of?" Joni asks in shock.

"He dreamt of a very tall building on fire and another tall building with a plane heading towards it."

Joni looks at her in concern.

"He says people are screaming and crying all around it," Steph adds.

Joni sees Joe getting up. He runs towards them all and throws himself at his mum.

"Joe, I've just told Miss Nicholls of your dream," she informs him.

"It's not a dream. It's real," he shouts to her.

Joni looks at them, in silence, unsure whether to even attempt to try to convince Joe to come into the classroom.

"Sometimes his dreams come true," Noah tells her.

Joni looks at Noah with interest, just nodding at him, lost for words.

"They do," adds Steph. "I'm very worried for today!"

"We'll take you all to Mr Morris," Joni tells them.

Steph nods and they all walk off. Joni gestures to Mrs Morton she will be straight back.

The children are now working in their places and Joni is helping Connor. Joe is absent. Jim comes to the door and Joni walks over to him.

"I've sent Joe home to sleep it off today and start again tomorrow," he whispers. "He's very distressed and tired."

Joni nods in understanding.

Joni is alone in her classroom at break time, with the children on the playground. Tracy enters. Joni looks up, disinterested.

"I hear how well Jonah is doing. What's brought that about?"

"He goes by Joe now," Joni blankly replies.

"I saw him in a terrible state this morning. Is he okay?"

Joni looks at her with an expression to show she does not intend to give much away.

"He is doing really well and I'm really proud of him," she states.

"What was wrong?"

"He'd had a dream that upset him."

Tracy stares at her, sensing her not impressed with the prying.

"Same thing happened when he was in my class. He dreamed he'd excreted out a bone and was hysterical about being missing one of his bones."

"It was probably to do with losing his grandad," Joni states in a very matter of fact tone. "Maybe it was metaphoric? He had lost something he needed."

Tracy nods to her.

"Oh, it could have been."

"You never mentioned he'd lost his grandad," Joni states, staring at her. "I wish I'd known."

They exchange glances.

2021

Joni hears Stacey, Jake and Luke enter downstairs. She closes the diary and smiles reminiscently. She then gets up to leave.

Heading downstairs, she hears they are in the kitchen, and she goes to join them.

"Hi, you lot," she lovingly states as she sees them.

"Hi," they all reply, in unison.

Without hesitation, Jake questions her.

"So, mum, what was Joe like at school?"

Joni and Stacey exchange glances.

"He was an interesting little boy. He was very bright. A genius."

"He's definitely a genius!"

"What do you know of him now, Jake?" she asks.

"There are three of them in the band. Joe is the lead singer. His brother, Noah, plays guitar. There's also Toby. He plays guitar too. Jonah writes the bulk of their stuff."

Stacey nods with interest.

"So, you really taught him?" Luke asks, still dubious.

"Yes. You've no idea how amazing this is for me."

"Well, we know he's alive and well," Stacey adds. "And that he's done very well for himself. Good to see he's using his talents."

"What else do you know about him?" Joni asks Jake.

Jake looks at her, unsure what else there would be to know.

"Is he married? Does he have children?"

Jake shrugs his shoulders.

"You can google it," he adds.

"I did but there's no actual information about him on the net other than he's based here in London."

"Could we see them in concert?" Jake asks.

"If they play here in London, we could try to get tickets."

Stacey nods to agree to that.

"Excellent," shouts Jake in excitement.

"I'll get them playing in concert up on YouTube," Jake says whilst getting the remote control and pressing it to find Indigo Joe in concert.

Joni looks up at the screen, in amazement, to see Joe and the band playing so well in a live performance.

"Oh, Joe," she says as she watches, emotion overcoming her.

Stacey smiles to her.

"I know how much this means," he says as he takes her hand and watches with her.

Now, evening, Joni's returns to her spare room and picks up her diary. She turns to the page headed: 'Tuesday 11th September 2001'.

"The day of 9/11," she says as she swallows and reads on.

47

2001

The children enter the classroom. Joe walks in with them, chatting happily to others.

Steph heads towards Joni.

"Is he ok?" Joni asks.

"Yes. He's all fine now."

"Good. We missed him yesterday. Good to have him back. He seems happy today."

"He is," Steph says. "But I'm so worried."

"I'm also worried for Joe," Joni tells her.

Steph looks at her, confused.

"Not for Jonah."

Joni looks confused.

"I'm not worried for him," Steph states clearly. "I'm worried for all those poor people in that building. It's a premonition. I just know it. But I have no way of preventing it, not knowing where it is."

Joni nods in bewilderment.

"Something is going to happen today," Steph continues.

"I'll keep a good eye on Joe today, and I'll catch you this afternoon at the end of the day to let you know how he's been."

"Thank you," Steph smiles.

Joni is at the front of the class with the children sat around her on the carpet area as they listen to her explain the timetable of the day.

Joe is sat with his head hung down.

"Today's lesson is all about communication through illustration," Joni says with a big smile, focused on Joe. "We will draw to communicate our thoughts. No talking or writing, just drawing."

Joe sits bolt upright and smiles at Joni.

"Sometimes no words are needed, and we can present our thoughts in pictures just as clearly," Joni adds.

Joe waves his hand and Joni nods to him.

"This is great that we can draw our thoughts but 'communication through illustration' goes beyond just drawing."

Joni nods to show understanding, although is a little confused.

THIRTEEN

The children are on the carpet area, each in pairs with their picture in their hands.

Joni addresses them.

"In your pairs, you are to show each other your picture and guess what each other's is."

The children talk in their pairs about their pictures.

After a few minutes, Joni asks them to come together again. She asks if anyone guessed, and virtually all put their hands up.

"Let's have one or two show their pictures to the class," Joni tells them.

Some hands go up and Joni points to Kai. He shows a picture with lots of people and a cake. Many shoot up their hand. Joni nods at Aisha.

"A birthday," she suggests.

Kai nods to show she is correct.

"One more," Joni says, looking around, nodding to Ben.

He holds up a picture of a lady, very pretty. They all shoot up their hand. Joni looks on in confusion that they would all know what this represents. She looks at them to all answer.

"Miss Nicholls," they all say together and Ben nods.

"Not a monster this time," Joe laughs. They all laugh too. Joni smiles with endearment as she looks around.

"We've a few minutes until lunch. Maybe I'll read a few pages of our story?"

Joe's hand shoots up and Joni looks at him to speak.

"Can I read a story from the library in my mind?"

"That's a lovely idea," she smiles to him.

Joe jumps up to the front of the class.

At lunchtime, Joni stands at the window, watching the children on the playground.

Joe is telling more stories, and many children are sat around him. They watch him avidly whilst he acts them out, smiling and laughing. Joe is enjoying his attention.

Joni smiles with enormous happiness to see this.

Joni is with Jim, in his office.

"It's great to hear that he's began interacting," Jim says with genuine kindness.

"I can't say how much."

"With interacting being a struggle to him, let's hope he can build on this storytelling."

"I had to share the good news."

"I'm so glad you did," Jim tells her. "Please, always do." He pauses and then jogs his own memory. "I'm glad you're here. Here's some information about your course on Thursday."

Jim passes Joni some papers.

"Thank you," she says as she glances over them.

"Also," Jim adds. "The student will be with you on Wednesday afternoon this week."

Joni nods to show she has taken in all the information.

"No worries. I'll look after her."

Now home time, the children get their coats and bags. A group of girls start to argue and Milly bursts into tears.

Joni goes straight over.

"Milly has stolen that coat," Chloe announces as Joni is close.

"I haven't," Milly shouts at Chloe. "It's mine."

Joni looks at them to stop and to listen to her.

"Milly, did you bring the coat in this morning?"

Milly doesn't answer.

"Milly," Joni repeats.

"No, but I found it."

"She found it in lost property," Chloe interrupts. "So, it's someone else's and they will be looking for it."

Joni looks directly at Milly.

"Is it from lost property?"

Milly nods her head with an annoyed look on her face.

Joe runs over, clearly annoyed.

"That's stealing," he shouts. "It's wrong to steal."

"Milly is going to do the right thing and put it back," Joni tells them all.

Joe looks angrily at Joni.

Joni turns to Milly.

"Milly, off you go."

Milly walks towards the door with the coat in her hand.

Joe kicks the wall.

Joni walks straight over and looks directly at him.

"Joe! That is not acceptable. You've had a brilliant day. Don't change that now."

Joe looks up, surprised.

"Have I had a brilliant day?" he asks.

"Yes. Your best one yet," Joni tells him.

Joe walks off with a smile. He then turns around.

"Sorry that I kicked the wall."

Joni nods to accept the apology.

The secretary comes into the classroom and walks over to Joni. She gestures to speak quietly to her.

Joni goes to her.

"There's an emergency meeting in the staffroom after school has finished," she whispers to Joni. "All staff must go straight there as soon as the children have gone."

Joni looks at her with concern.

"What's happened?" she asks, startled.

The secretary looks at Joni with genuine fear.

"The world is under attack."

Joni pauses, studying her.

"What? What do you mean?" Joni stutters.

"Well, America is under attack. You must go immediately."

"I will," Joni informs her.

"To warn you, parents may be distressed," the secretary adds.

Joni nods at her to show she understands, with a fearful look in her eyes.

The parents chat frantically and collect the children quicker than usual. There is panic in the atmosphere.

Steph rushes up to Joni.

Joni looks to her in confusion.

"There's been an attack in America," Steph informs Joni, her voice shaking. "A plane has flown into the Twin Towers. There's total devastation."

Joni and Steph hold each other's stare, eyes wide. Steph waits for Joni to react, but Joni stands silent with shock.

"This is bigger, much bigger, than I had thought," Steph says, holding back tears. "I want to get straight back to see the news."

Joni nods at her, still stunned, and then looks to Joe who has a questioning expression.

"I'll explain to Joe at home."

Joni nods again.

"Are you okay?" she asks Steph.

Steph shrugs, too shocked to answer.

"I'll catch you tomorrow," Steph says.

"Yes. Tomorrow."

She then leaves quickly with a confused Joe following her.

Joni walks into the staffroom but stays by the door. Everyone is watching a television placed there of the news footage. The images show a plane flying into the Twin Towers, the first tower collapsing and the devastation through New York.

There is a deathly silence as everyone remains watching the television, open mouthed.

Jim walks by Joni at the entrance and they catch each other's gaze.

"Can I see you?" she asks him.

Jim nods towards the door and walks back through it. He is wobbly on his walking stick.

Joni follows him to just outside the door, away from the earshot of others.

Jim looks directly at Joni with a face of shock.

"Joe Huckle predicted this," she whispers but with direct eye contact.

Jim shakes his head.

"Not now, Joni. Not now. This is all too much to take in, let alone with Joe in the equation."

Joni nods in acceptance.

Jim walks into the staffroom, to the front. He turns down the volume of the television and addresses everyone.

"I'm sending you all home. You can watch the news there. We'll meet tomorrow morning here in the staffroom, 8.15am prompt."

People start to get up. Joni freezes and stares at Jim. Jim notices her gaze and looks back at her. They hold their stare.

FOURTEEN

Joni walks into her flat, shuts the door behind her and walks to her living room. Still in shock, she sits down on her sofa, puts her head into her hands and stares into space.

Later, Shirley is with her in her flat. They watch the events on the television together.

"I do believe he predicted it," Joni states.

Shirley stares at her, taking it in, and thinking before she speaks.

"I want to say something here that I feel is important."

Joni nods for her to continue.

"It's not about whether he predicted it or not. No one can say whether he did or didn't. It's going to be about how it's handled."

Joni nods to agree.

"A good point," she tells Shirley.

They both look back to the television, each in their own thoughts.

"I'd advise two things," Shirley announces. "Firstly, let him talk. Let him express himself."

Joni nods with full eye contact.

"Secondly, his mum is going to believe he did, so I'd advise to just listen to her. Sometimes people just want to be listened to. There's nothing more you can do."

Joni smiles in agreement.

"That's invaluable advice. Thank you. It's just such a disrupted week. I'm out of the class on Thursday for a course and I've got a student teacher in my classroom tomorrow afternoon."

Shirley laughs out loud.

"That's a baptism of fire for a student, a day after this. Do you know anything about them?"

Joni shakes her head.

"I know nothing about her other than she has been placed with the older years for two weeks but is coming to me for a comparison."

Joni pauses, deep in thought.

"But these aside, I'm nervous for tomorrow. I'm not sure what to expect from the aftermath of these attacks."

Shirley pulls an expression to empathise.

"Tomorrow won't be easy," Shirley states.

"What's your advice?"

Shirley pauses.

"Be honest. Simple, but honest. Go with the flow. You'll do well."

Joni looks back at her, not so certain.

The clock shows it is late into the night and Joni is playing pool in her living room. In an unsettled mood, she hits the balls harder than usual.

2021

Joni, Stacey, Jake and Luke are all at the kitchen table, watching the news report on the twentieth anniversary of 9/11 being tomorrow.

"Do you want to see Indigo Joe's new song?" interrupts Jake.

They all look at him with interest.

"Oh, let's see," Joni says with excitement.

"Definitely!" exclaims Stacey. "Do you think it will do well?"

"Yes," Jake informs him. "It will top the sales charts."

"Wow," says Joni, overjoyed and amazed.

Jake picks up the remote control and switches it to YouTube. They all look to the television screen in their kitchen to watch 'Change the World' by Indigo Joe.

I turned on my TV
More blood on my screen
Wars won but lives lost
High debts for low costs

I look at the state of the world today
And me, I'll blame the governments
But I wonder what I'd do
If I were in their shoes

Could I really change the world?
Could I really change the world?
Could I really change the world?
Stand up and not outsell
Could I really change the world?

Stacey and Joni watch the screen in wonder.

"He does write clever songs," Stacey states.

"He does but, that isn't surprising. He was a very clever boy."

Later, back in her spare room, Joni takes out the diary and turns to the page headed: 'Wednesday 12th September 2001'.

"Another day I'll never forget," she says to herself.

2001

Joni knocks on Jim's door. He glances up at her from his desk and smiles. He then gets up and pulls out a chair.

Joni walks in, closes the door and sits down. She then looks to Jim to begin the conversation.

"Thank you for coming. I was going to come to you in a moment."

Joni nods to show she is listening, still allowing for him to speak.

"I didn't mean to be dismissive yesterday. I was in shock."

"I totally understand," Joni tells him. "We all were."

"I've not really slept," Jim confides. "But I'm not sure if I've given more thought to the events in America or to Joe Huckle."

Joni nods to agree.

"I'm a logical man, Joni. I have a solution for everything. But for the first time, I'm not overly sure of the answer here myself."

"Because there is no answer," Joni states.

Jim ponders it over.

"Maybe that's the only logic in this."

"My suggestion to you in this is to just ask the questions," Joni puts to him. "I advise this when speaking to the Huckles."

Jim studies Joni with interest.

Joni smiles at him.

"Listen to 'their' answers. You don't have to agree, but don't disagree. I think just listening to them and accepting that their view is their view, is the right way forward."

Jim looks at Joni with admiration.

"That is great advice. Thank you, Joni. I'll try to listen instead of lead."

Jim pauses, thoughtfully.

"Do you know I nearly retired this year? I spent most of the night wishing I had."

"Can't say I blame you," Joni jovially replies.

"I'm too old for all of this. It's a younger person's game, the teaching profession. Teaching is changing, the world is changing and I'm just ageing."

"Do 'you' believe it could have been some type of premonition?" Joni asks him.

Jim shrugs.

"He didn't say where or when. He didn't give specific details. It could be an enormous coincidence."

"Do you think there's a possibility?"

Jim thinks before replying but chooses to confide.

"When he was in my office, talking of his dream, he was very convincing. There are cross overs and with the timing, I think he may have sensed something."

Joni nods in appreciation of his trust.

"I think so too."

Jim stares at Joni, in deep thought.

"When my daughter was applying to universities, she wanted Exeter first and London was her second choice. I knew she'd end up in London. I don't know why I felt that, but I just did. She did end up in London. Maybe, my daughter is so important to me that I sensed what would happen to her."

Jim pauses, thoughtfully.

"It must be a similar thing, a natural intuition," he continues. "Children with autistic traits can be very intuitive and perceptive, and Joe does possibly have such traits."

"Do you think he's psychic?" Joni asks.

"He won't be the first. They say such people start sensing things as children."

Jim stares ahead, deep in thought.

"A worry I have is for this becoming a topic of debate among staff. We'll keep the dream and its details between ourselves."

"I agree."

Joni and Jim look at each other.

"So," Jim states to take the lead, "The plan is that I'll call mum and ask them to come to your classroom fifteen minutes earlier than usual. I'll be there too. We'll all talk."

"We'll listen," Joni adds humorously.

Jim laughs in amusement.

FIFTEEN

Joni walks back to her classroom, passing Mrs Morton in the corridor.

"Hi. You're early today," she greets her.

"I wanted to hear Jim speak this morning," she tells Joni.

Joni nods to show she understands this wish. She then moves nearer to Mrs Morton.

"Can you keep a close eye on Joe today?" she whispers.

Mrs Morton nods.

"Maybe take him outside for a while. Let him speak and draw about it if he wants to. I've no idea what to expect from him today."

Mrs Morton nods again.

Tracy walks by and they nod to each other to say hello. Joni waits for Tracy to be out of sight.

"Can you keep the details of the dream to yourself?" she whispers to Mrs Morton. "It's only the two of us, and Jim, that know the details. I don't want it getting out and it becoming debated as to whether he did or didn't predict it."

Mrs Morton pulls an expression of seriousness.

"I totally understand, and I won't say a word."

Mrs Morton pauses in thought.

"Do you think he did?" she asks Joni.

Joni shrugs her shoulders.

"We'll never know. I think it's possible. I think all that matters is how we handle it."

"You're right about that. I'll go with whatever you advise."

Joni smiles to her, respect and gratitude.

"I think we just let him speak and listen to him."

"I agree. Good advice. Thank you, Joni."

Joni smiles again.

"Thank you for all your support. I couldn't do it without you."

Mrs Morton beams.

Joni enters the staffroom. It is full but unusually silent.

Everyone turns to listen avidly as Jim addresses them.

"Hi everyone. I'm going to keep this brief so you can get back to your classes."

57

Everyone waits. Jim pauses.

"Yesterday, in the United States, four planes were hijacked, and purposely crashed, for the aim of causing devastation. This has caused a very high death toll and uncertainty now for the world. I do believe we may face some sad times ahead and we cannot know the impact upon the world at this time. For now, we can only focus on the children in our school and how any of this may affect them. I ask you to work on or off timetable, as necessary, but begin your day with an open discussion regarding what has happened."

Jim pauses as everyone nods to agree.

"Be mindful some will have seen the news in detail and others not at all. I'll walk around to see you all in turn and am available wherever needed. I'll hold an assembly at 9.30am so please be in the hall for then. Thank you for listening."

Jim walks out of the staffroom with an expression of sadness and without making eye contact with anyone. He again seems unsteady on his stick. The staff let him exit in silence, smiling respectfully at him as he does.

Joe, Noah and Steph enter Joni's classroom, accompanied by the secretary. Jim and Joni are at a table but get up to greet them, pulling out chairs.

"Hello," Steph enthusiastically announces. "Thank you so much for asking us to come. I wanted a chance to talk."

"How are you all? How's Joe?" Joni asks.

Joe shrugs his shoulders but smiles happily.

"He's okay," Steph replies. "We're all okay."

"Did you 'all' watch the news last night?" Jim asks.

"Yes, we 'all' watched it," Steph informs him. "On something so massive in the world, I think it's best that the boys see it and then are aware of what any discussions are referring to. Some things you can keep from them and some you can't. If you can't, you just be truthful."

Jim nods in agreement.

"How were you all whilst watching it?" Jim asks.

"They were the buildings in my dream," Joe quietly tells them.

"You certainly described them very well, Joe," Jim states.

Joe, Noah and Steph all look shocked.

"You believe him?" Steph asks. "You believe it was a premonition? You believe he saw what was going to happen?"

"I know Miss Nicholls believes me," Joe interrupts before he can answer.

Joni looks directly at Joe and smiles empathetically.

"Joe, you described the events very well."

Steph and Joe turn to each other and smile in disbelief.

"Joe," Jim says directly to him to get his attention. "This is something that happens more often than you think."

"I said this," Noah interrupts. "You hear of it all the time and people do this as their jobs."

"I had another dream last night," Joe announces.

Joni and Jim turn to Joe, wide eyed, silent for him to explain further.

"It was how it's going to look after," he tells them.

"Wow!" Jim states with clear interest.

"How did it look, Joe?" asks Joni.

Joe pauses to check he has everyone's full attention.

"They didn't build the buildings again. They leave it flat."

"Tell them more," Steph tells Joe.

Joe looks to his mum.

She nods to confirm it's okay to.

"Everyone who died has their name written on it. It's peaceful. The people are happy in the garden of light and happy their name is there, engraved in statues forever."

"Joe, that's a lovely ending," Joni says, barely audible through her emotion. "It makes me happy to know that. I've always wanted to see New York. I'll visit when it's all cleared to see it just how you've described it."

Joni looks to Jim for his reply.

"Joe, you have a gift you can use to help people and make people happy."

Joe beams an enormous smile.

Joe turns to Joni.

"Can I tell the class about my dream last night to make them feel happier?"

"Of course," she smiles gently to him.

"Joe, I've been teaching a long time," Jim adds. "When you get to my age, and you meet a boy as gifted as you, you know your whole career was worthwhile. Teaching is a privilege in any lifetime but moments like this are special and will never be forgotten. I've learnt something today from you, Joe."

Steph bursts into tears.

"Sorry, I've dreamed of the day my son could be himself at school."

There is a silence and Joni catches Joe's attention.

"Just be yourself, Joe. Follow your heart. Never be afraid to do either," she tells him.

"Okay," he replies.

"Tell them about our band," Noah whispers to him.

Joe faces everyone square on.

"We started our band last night with our music teacher and his son called Toby."

"Wow. A band. That's fantastic," Joni states in amazement.

"We have named the band Indigo Joe," Joe tells them all. "Mum says everyone has light around them and everyone's light is a different colour. Mum says my colour is indigo so it's my favourite colour. So, I'm Indigo Joe and so is my band."

"It's a lovely name for a band," Joni says with genuine interest. "What colour is Noah?"

"Noah is red," Steph replies instantly. "He's a very grounded person."

Noah shakes his head, bemused by it all, and smiles.

"Indigo Joe sounded better than Red Noah," he laughs.

Jim and Joni laugh.

"Joe will be the main singer anyway so it's best if it is about him," Noah adds.

"Can you sing?" Joni asks Joe.

"Nearly as good as I can draw," he replies. "But not quite that good yet."

"I'd love to hear you sing," Joni adds.

"I never do anything until I can do it properly."

Joni nods to show she understands.

"We just have to accept that's how Joe is," Noah tells Joni.

"We do accept Joe and how he is," Joni reassures Joe.

"And this is why he's doing so well," adds Steph.

"Accepting is the key here," Jim confirms. "Accepting what we cannot change, accepting different opinions and differences in people."

Other children have begun to gather at the classroom door.

"I'm going to open the door in a moment," Joni says to them. "But thank you to all three of you for coming in. It's been a lovely conversation."

"Thank you to you both," Steph tells them with direct eye contact and genuine gratitude. "You've both changed my world. And Jonah's too."

Joe nods in agreement.

SIXTEEN

The children enter the classroom, put their things away and sit down in front of Joni. Connor enters with his mum. He is completely bald.

"He's a bit self-conscious of his new haircut," Connor's mum tells Joni. "I had no choice. It was the only way to properly get rid of the nits."

Joni smiles to Connor.

"It will soon grow back."

Joe bursts over.

"Connor, it looks really good," he interrupts.

Connor smiles at Joe.

The children are now sat around Joni in the classroom on the carpet area.

"Did anyone watch the news last night on television?" she asks them.

Several children put their hand up.

She nods to Ethan.

"I saw the planes going into the buildings and setting them on fire."

She smiles kindly to him and then nods at Chloe.

"I saw people jumping from the buildings."

Joni pulls a face of sadness and nods to show she has listened. She then nods to Lewis.

"People were screaming and running."

"There were big clouds of dust sweeping through the streets," Milly interrupts.

Joni gestures to Milly to raise her hand and looks at the children with a serious expression.

"Can I ask for hands up if you saw all this on the television last night?"

As most of the children have put their hand up but with no sign of distress, she proceeds.

"Sometimes bad things happen in the world," she tells them directly. They remain quiet as she pauses.

"How do we all feel today?" she continues.

Ben raises his hand and Joni nods to him to answer.

"A bit scared but not that scared because it didn't happen here."

Ethan raises his hand and Joni nods to him.

"Could it happen here?"

Joe furiously waves his hand to answer this for Ethan. Joni nods to him to answer.

"You don't need to worry about that," Joe informs him. "I had a dream about it happening and it only happened there, and it only happened the once."

Ethan smiles at him.

"Thank you, Joe," Joni says, taking back the lead. "Things like this don't happen again because people in the Government stop it from happening again."

Connor raises his hand and Joni nods to him.

"Will there be a war?"

Joni pauses. The children look at her to answer.

"Wars do happen around the world but there's no war here," she tells them. "We're all in a safe country."

"But will our army go and fight?" Caleb interrupts.

Joni gestures to him to show he must raise his hand.

"Sometimes, our army does fight in other wars," she answers.

Kai raises his hand and Joni nods.

"How can we make war stop?"

Joni shrugs her shoulders and holds out her hands.

"I wish I knew," she tells them. "I suppose people disagree all the time and when it's between countries, it becomes worse. Often, it's over land or resources such as oil."

Joni pauses and the children watch her in silence.

"Let's demonstrate. Aisha and Zain come to the front."

Both Aisha and Zain stand and walk over to where they were asked to.

Joni hands five pencils to Aisha and one to Zain. Zain pulls a face.

"Aisha is a country and Zain is a country."

The children laugh.

"Aisha has five pencils and Zain has one. How do they each feel?"

Several children put their hand up.

Joni nods to Kali.

"Aisha is happier than Zain."

"Yes," Joni agrees, nodding to Ethan.

"Zain may be jealous."

"Yes," Joni agrees. "What may Zain do when he is feeling jealous?"

Several raise their hands and Joni nods to Ben.

"He may try to take Aisha's."

"He may," Joni agrees. "What's Aisha going to do?"

Aisha enthusiastically waves her hand and Joni nods to her.

"I'm going to try to stop him and protect my pencils," she shouts with indignation.

"Yes," Joni agrees, nodding at Milly.

"Then they start fighting and it starts a war."

"That is one way it starts. People don't want to give up what they have and those without as much see this as unfair," Joni states. "Sometimes, those with five pencils want the one of the other. That, sadly, is how the world can also be," Joni tells them. "Arguments can get complicated and go back and forth. When someone feels wronged, they can want revenge. But that just leads to further problems, never solutions."

Mrs Morton catches Joni's eye contact and pulls a face to show she agrees.

The children look to her blankly with some confusion; Joni chooses not to persist.

"We have our own little wars here in our classroom," Joni reminds them.

Chloe raises her hand and Joni looks to her.

"Like when Milly took the coat."

"Yes," Joni says flatly, skimming over the comment. "What could we do about those?"

Joe shoots up his hand and Joni looks at him to answer.

"Everyone could try to be kind."

Joni nods to agree.

"After what happened yesterday, in the news, that would be a nice way to spend today."

Joni pauses to look at the children, all totally engaged.

"So," she continues. "Today, I want everyone to try their best to think of everyone else's feelings. We'll stop later to see who has done some nice things for others."

Joe puts up his hand and Joni nods at him to answer.

"I am going to tell more stories at break and lunch. If people are sad or worried, they can come to listen."

Several children nod enthusiastically.

Joe smiles at Joni and Joni smiles back at him.

Kali puts up her hand and Joni nods at her to speak.

"But why did someone want to fly a plane into a building?"

Joni takes a deep breath in before she answers.

"I don't know why somebody would want to do that. I don't understand that myself."

The children sit quietly and Joni smiles at them.

Kali raises her hand and Joni nods to her.

"My mum said they are still looking for people and that people are trapped."

"They are still finding people and still saving many lives," Joni replies.

"I had another dream last night," Joe announces. The children look to him to continue. "The people who died are okay in Heaven now, and the people who clear the rubble write all their names in statues and they are happy with this."

Joni smiles warmly to Joe and the children reciprocate this.

"Where are the statues?" asks Ethan.

"It's where the buildings were," Joe replies instantly. "They clear it all and then they flatten it and make it as a memory to all the people who died. It's peaceful. My mum says it's called a memorial."

The children listen avidly and smile at him.

"They do make memorials for people who died in wars," Ethan states in support.

"This is a memorial for those that died from the plane attacks," Joe confirms.

"Can people visit it?" Ethan asks.

"Yes," answers Joe assertively. "So good wins in the end."

"Good does," reassures Joni to them all. "Let's make today a day where we all look out for each other and do good things for each other."

The children nod to agree.

"Good always wins here too," she jovially adds.

Zain raises his hand and Joni nods to him.

"Something else happened yesterday," he tells her. "Something totally different to the plane attacks."

"What was that?" Joni asks.

"My dad had a va…va…tectomy," he mispronounces. "Because he doesn't want any more children."

Joni and Mrs Morton exchange glances but the children remain blank.

"I hope your dad is okay," Joni answers and changes the subject. "Actually, it's time for assembly. We have an assembly today for Mr Morris to talk to everyone about what happened yesterday in the news."

SEVENTEEN

Everyone is now in the school hall for assembly. Jim looks over to Joni as to ask if everything is okay.

She nods back.

Jim smiles, pleased. He then addresses the school.

"Good morning, all."

"Good morning, Mr Morris," the children reply in unison.

Jim pauses and the children wait in silence for him to speak.

"Yesterday was a very sad day. I know you've discussed this in your classes. I'm going to say that today is a day where we also need to see the beauty and good in the world. On the news, we saw people helping others, even risking their lives for others. We saw the bravery of the fire service. We saw the public helping each other. Whenever bad things happen, we see good; we see people pulling together and we see love."

The children all stare at Jim in silence as he reflects.

"When you watch the news tonight or at any point in the future, look for the good you see. Take this as a lesson in life. There is always good. You only need to look."

Jim again pauses as the children look on.

"I also need to mention another important issue and that is of milk," he announces.

Joni turns to Mrs Morton with an expression of bemusement.

"Only in a school would milk be as important," she whispers.

Mrs Morton smirks.

"There are straw wrappers from the milk cartons being left around school," he continues. "These need to be placed in a bin."

The children walk out of the classroom and onto the playground, for their break.

Milly, Lewis and Chloe approach Joe.

"Joe, can we hear your story?" asks Milly.

Joe nods enthusiastically, beaming at Joni.

The children are working at their tables. Joe had been outside briefly with Mrs Morton. He enters the classroom and walks over to Joni with a picture he has drawn. He holds it up in front of her; it is of people coming down from the Twin Towers in parachutes.

"Hi, Joe. This looks good."

"This is a design of how to make a change in the world to stop this happening again," he tells her enthusiastically. "Everyone who works on a high floor in a tall building should have a parachute pack that they can use if they need to escape. It's a bit like everyone on a plane has a life jacket for if the plane crashes in the sea."

Joni takes the picture to see it in more detail. She looks at it in amazement.

"That's a great idea. I only hope they make a change like this."

"They're special parachutes that open straight away because a normal parachute may not open in time," he continues to explain.

"It's a fantastic idea."

Joe breathes inwardly with an enormous smile.

Joni is at the front of the class and the children are sitting on the carpet in front of her.

"Before we go to lunch, can anyone tell me anything kind they did to make our world, our classroom, a better place this morning?"

Many hands go up. Joni nods at Aisha to speak.

"I gave my gloves to Kali because her hands were cold."

"That was very kind," Joni says as she nods at Ben.

"I said sorry to Lewis because I accidentally stood on his foot and then let him have the ball instead of arguing about it."

"Two great things. Well done," Joni replies as she nods at Milly.

"I'm never going to take anything from lost property ever again."

Everyone laughs endearingly.

"I'm very happy to hear that," Joni states as she nods at Kali.

"I looked for people who were lonely at breaktime and let them play with me and my friends."

"That's a lovely one," Joni states as she nods at Chloe.

"I let people use my rubber because I don't usually like sharing. But also, I really like Joe's parachute idea and his plan to save people in the future."

"I do too," Joni smiles to her as she nods at Ethan.

"I'm going to listen to one of Joe's stories at lunch because I am really proud of him for improving his behaviour."

"We're all proud of Joe for improving his behaviour, aren't we?" she asks the class.

The children nod to agree and start to clap.

Joe beams with pride as he watches.

<u>2021</u>

Joni closes her diary and leaves her spare room. She walks down her stairs and into a room with her old pool table in it. She smiles to see it.

She then walks into her kitchen area to see Stacey, Jake and Luke. They are watching the video for 'Change the World' by Indigo Joe. Joni looks up to the screen, in awe.

I turned on my TV
Species lost, cut trees
More crime and pollution
With no cure or solution

I look at the state of the world today
And wonder where the good news has all gone
But if I'd the chance to put things right
How would I not go wrong?

Could I really change the world?
Could I really change the world?
Could I really change the world?
Stand up and not outsell
Could I really change the world?

It's just of our wonderful world we abuse
Have you ever felt fed up with the news?

So, I turned off my TV
Too much already seen
Animal rights, the environment
Human life and corruption

I look at the state of the world today
And me, I'll blame the governments
But I wonder what I'd do
If I were in their shoes

Could I really change the world?
Could I really change the world?
Could I really change the world?
Stand up and not outsell
Could I really change the world?

I wonder what I'd do
If I were in their shoes

"Oh, Joe," Joni states emotionally. "You are truly talented."

"That was a brilliant song," Stacey tells them all.

They all nod to agree.

"An interesting political stance and good point to make," Stacey adds.

They all pause to think of what Stacey has said.

Joni turns to Jake and Luke.

"Do you know, boys, that 9/11 happened when Joe was in my class?" Joni rhetorically asks them.

Jake and Luke look directly at her.

"I saw a programme not that long ago where people were saying where they were that day," Jake answers. "It was very interesting. Were you in your classroom?"

Joni nods to him to reply.

He pulls an expression of interest.

"The attacks happened early afternoon, but we had remained in our own bubble as a class, not being informed until the end of the school day. I imagine most heads took that decision."

Jake listens with keen interest.

"It was the day after that was a tough day for teachers."

"I can imagine," says Jake with empathy.

"That was certainly a day I've never forgotten," states Stacey.

"You've not forgotten the day after?" asks Jake in slight confusion as to why.

"I most definitely haven't!" Stacey exclaims.

"Why? Where were you, dad?" Jake questions in the hope he'll reveal.

Joni and Stacey look at each other in amusement.

"I was in your mum's classroom."

Jake and Luke look at each other with interest.

"Why?" asks Luke.

"What were you doing there?" adds Jake.

Stacey and Joni again look at each other in amusement.

"Actually, boys, that's where we met!" Joni declares.

"You met dad in your classroom?" Jake asks.

Joni laughs.

"I did!"

EIGHTEEN

Joni walks back into her classroom after lunch and is startled to see a man standing in there.

"Hello?" Joni asks inquisitively.

"Hi. I'm Stacey," he says as he walks over to her. She notices he is attractive and has a big smile. He is smartly dressed in a shirt and tie. He extends his arm, and they shake hands.

"Hi, Stacey," Joni replies. "Was I expecting you?"

"I'm the student in your class this afternoon."

Joni looks at him with a pleasant surprise.

"Oh."

There is an awkward moment of silence, broken by Stacey.

"You looked shocked. I hope you were expecting me."

"Sort of."

Stacey looks at her with a confused expression.

"I didn't realise you were going to be a man. I thought you would be a girl."

"That's the joys of a unisex name," Stacey states.

Joni smiles to him in appreciation of the response a name can cause.

"A man in the class will be great."

Stacey nods with an expression of bemusement.

"I'm Joni. Joni Nicholls," she tells him as she points to her name badge on her lanyard.

Stacey extends his arm to shake hands again.

"I'm Mr Polanski, in class," he answers with a smile.

Joni and Stacey shake hands.

"Hello, Mr Polanski, in class," she smiles. "I apologise for just now. Let's start again."

Stacey nods to accept.

"It's strange that I haven't seen you around. How have the older years been?"

"A challenge. But good. I'm looking forward to an easier afternoon."

Joni pauses and throws him a look of amused irritation.

"Easier?"

69

"Yes. Here with the little ones. Easier."

Joni studies him.

"You're in for a shock, Mr Polanski," Joni directly informs him. "Don't underestimate the thought capacity of a six-year-old. They are at their peak of being inquisitive."

Stacey looks unconvinced. He then points to a guitar in the corner of the room.

"I've brought my guitar. Would you be happy for me to play a song?"

Joni nods with enthusiasm.

"Oh, wow. That will be lovely. The children will love that."

Stacey smiles to her.

"Can I ask if there are any children to look out for?"

"A little boy called Joe who can be highly sensitive," she informs him. "He's gifted but easily upset."

Joni walks to the window where she sees Joe surrounded by children.

"That's him, telling stories to the others," she tells Stacey as she points to Joe's direction.

Stacey walks over to the window to see him.

"He's quite the entertainer."

"That's very recent. It's a way of getting the others to spend time with him. He has been quite lonely."

Stacey nods with an empathetic look.

"He could do with a positive male role model."

Stacey looks at her with amusement.

"I'll do my best."

"I look forward to it," Joni jovially replies.

Stacey smiles in amusement and gives her a look of interest.

The children come in from lunch. They look startled to see Stacey.

Joe stops to see him, stares at him and frowns, in disapproval.

"Who's that?" Caleb shouts out.

"Why is he in here?" Kali asks.

"If everyone can sit down, and I'll explain after the register."

Mrs Morton walks in, pleasantly surprised to see Stacey.

"This is Stacey, our student. Mr Polanski, in class," Joni introduces him to Mrs Morton.

The children are sat on the carpet in front of Joni.

Joe has his head in his lap, hiding his face.

"For this afternoon, and only this afternoon, we have a visitor to our class," Joni tells the children. "This is Mr Polanski. He has been working with the older children, but he's come to see us this afternoon. So, I want everyone to remember how we are being kind to make our world better, and to show Mr Polanski what a fantastic class we are."

Connor raises his hand and Joni nods to him to answer.

"Is he going to teach us or just watch?"

"He's going to join in and help, but he has brought his guitar to play some music with us all later," Joni informs them in reply.

Joe looks around the room. His eyes catch Stacey's guitar; they then move back and forth to the guitar and to Stacey.

Ethan puts up his hand and Joni nods to him.

"Can we play 'Ask the teacher' with Mr Polanski?"

"Oh, no," Joni interjects. "We won't subject poor Mr…" she tails off, deep in thought. Joni pauses with a mischievous smile on her face.

"Hands up to ask questions to Mr Polanski."

Joni looks at Stacey and smirks slightly flirtatiously. Joni gestures for him to take her chair at the front.

He walks over and sits down, with a look of apprehension.

The children start to put their hands up.

"Easier?" she whispers to Stacey with a giggle.

Stacey and Joni exchange glances.

Stacey points at Milly to ask.

"Did you teach my sister?"

"Who is your sister?" Stacey asks.

"Ellie in Year 6!" she exclaims as though he should know.

"I did teach an Ellie in Year 6."

"She said that you are funny," Milly continues.

"I'll try my best."

Stacey points at Chloe.

"Do you have a hamster?"

"No. I don't have a hamster."

Stacey points at Ethan.

"Do you have a goldfish or a piranha?"

"Neither."

Stacey points at Aisha.

"Do you have a cat?"

"No."

Stacey points at Zain.

"Do you have a dog?"

"No. I don't actually have any pets at all."

Aisha bursts into uncontrollable tears.

Stacey glares towards Joni but she gestures him to ask her.

"Are you okay?"

"My dog died, and Zain just reminded me," Aisha shouts emotionally.

"I'm sorry to hear," Stacey tells her empathetically. "How long ago?"

"He died last night," she replies. "We forgot to feed him."

"You forgot to feed him!" Stacey replies quickly in shock.

"It's a Tamagotchi. It's not a real dog," Milly shouts out.

Stacey turns to Joni.

"What's a Tamagotchi?" he asks.

"A cyber pet."

"That's good," states a relieved Stacey. "I was worried for a moment."

"Good!" shouts an indignant Aisha.

"I mean, it's good that it's not a real dog," he explains.

Aisha folds her arms and scowls.

Stacey pauses, baffled, but pointing to Lewis.

"Is the tooth fairy real?"

"Of course."

"Then why does she give more money to some children than others?" persists Lewis.

Stacey looks at Joni to answer. She gestures it's for him to answer with an encouraging smile. The children stare at Stacey to continue.

"Maybe it just depends on how much money she has at the time. Or some nights there may be more children to share it between. It's luck of the draw. Life's a bit like that. Let's keep these questions coming," he smiles to Joni.

NINETEEN

Joni smiles to Stacey for his answer, displaying respect for him.

The children notice and smile in reciprocation to Mr Polanski.

Joe turns to Joni and smirks to show he has caught on she's testing him.

Stacey smiles to them both and pulls a face to suggest he can rise to the challenge.

Joni sees the children with their hands up to ask more questions.

"Keep the questions coming," she repeats Stacey's words to them.

Stacey points to Kai.

"How much money do you have?"

"I'm not rich but I'm not poor. I'm buying a house. I worked hard to save the money I needed for it. I suggest you all work hard at school and get good jobs to buy your own house and get a top car too," he replies as he points to Ben.

"Do you drive fast?"

"I'm a law-abiding citizen and drive within the speed limits."

The children laugh. Stacey looks confused as to why it was funny, but points to Kali.

"Can a man marry another man?"

"Yes," he says, pointing to Joe.

"Do you have a wife?"

"Not yet."

Joe turns to Joni and looks at her with a face of interest.

Stacey has already pointed to Lewis, having clocked Joe's thought process.

"Do you have grandchildren?"

"How old do you think I am?"

"One hundred and two," Lewis laughs, and the children laugh with him.

Stacey laughs too, pointing at Chloe.

"What's your name again?"

"Mr Polanski. It's Polish. My grandad came over from Poland in the Second World War and stayed," he expands, pointing to Ethan.

"Is there going to be another war?"

Stacey pauses to ponder his answer.

"Why do you think there may be a war?"

73

"Because of the planes going into the buildings. Did you see it?"

Stacey looks at Joni in a poignant way.

"I did. It's very sad. We must hope there isn't going to be a war. But if there is a war, it will be a long way away in another country."

Stacey points to Connor.

"Was it Indian people like Aisha that started it?"

The children are all silent and stare at Stacey to answer.

A look of being challenged sweeps across Stacey's face.

Joni looks at him to suggest she can take over, but Stacey ignores it.

"No. No. It wasn't. It wasn't any race of people or any religion. People from the same country or religion as the people who did this, wouldn't want to be connected to this. We must never think like that."

Stacey smiles warmly to Connor and all the children. "We must all support each other," he adds.

Joni looks at him, touched by his response.

Stacey points to Milly.

"Did you see the dust covering the streets?"

"I did see the news footage showing that. It was more rubble than dust."

"What's the difference?" Milly asks further.

"Dust is what we get around our houses. That's why we dust, to remove the dust that collects and keep them clean. Who dusts their house for their mum?"

The children shake their heads and laugh.

"Dust in our houses is actually a mix of bits of fibres from materials around us, such as our clothes, blankets and carpets, as well as old, dead skin cells we have shed."

The children pull faces of disgust.

"Did you know we are like a snake?"

The children laugh.

Joni smiles at him to show she is impressed with his handling of the questions.

"We shed our skin all the time too, just like a snake does."

The children all pull faces.

"Although, a snake sheds the whole lot at once and we shed little bits at a time called cells. Each skin cell is so small we can't see it. But we're shedding our skin, and growing new skin under it, all the time. The bits we shed, collect and make dust."

The children stare wide eyed at Stacey, engrossed.

"But the 'dust' you saw on the news coverage is all part of the building. Broken parts of buildings are called rubble."

Joe puts up his hand and Stacey points to him, smiling to see he has gained his trust.

"What is stardust?"

"Now, there's a question!" Stacey exclaims. "It can mean something is magical. If you sprinkle something with stardust, you hope it becomes magical. Though, building on this, do you know of the 'Big Bang' theory?"

The children shake their heads as they avidly listen.

"This is the belief that everything, including our planet, and its plants and creatures, have evolved from a star exploding. If this is correct, and the world evolved from an exploding star, we are all stardust."

"Was Heaven made too when this star exploded?" Joe asks, wide-eyed.

"Everything was made then so I guess Heaven would have been too."

"What do you think Heaven looks like?" Joe asks Stacey.

Stacey pauses, sensing his answer of great importance to Joe.

"I imagine it being very peaceful and white."

Joe turns to Joni, eyes wide. Stacey observes this and smiles at Joni. He then looks back at Joe.

"It is peaceful and white," Joe declares. "I know. And it's full of light."

"Now, light is also interesting. Shall I tell you all about light?" Stacey asks them.

The children all nod enthusiastically, especially Joe.

"There's a secret about light. People think that you can't see light, but light splits into a rainbow. This can be seen if you hold a crystal up in the sun. This will split the light, and you'll see a rainbow up on the wall."

The children stare at him in awe.

"Shall we challenge your teacher here to buy a crystal at the weekend and demonstrate this to you next week?" Stacey asks the class, looking at Joni with a cheeky smirk.

The children nod enthusiastically at Joni.

She nods back in agreement, and to Stacey with a smile.

"This also happens in the sky after rain. The sun shines on the rain. That too splits the light, and you see a rainbow up in the sky."

Joni looks out of the window, up to a clear, blue sky without any rainbows.

"I really like light," Joe tells Stacey and the class.

"If you like light, you may like Diwali, the festival of light. This is to give thanks for light. No one would want to live in the dark."

The children stare at Stacey, totally engaged.

"What are the colours of the rainbow?" Joe asks him.

"Red, orange, yellow, green, blue, indigo and violet."

"Indigo," Joe shouts out. "My band is called Indigo Joe."

"Wow, you're in a band?" Stacey asks him.

"Yes," states Joe.

"What do you play?" Stacey continues the conversation.

"My brother plays guitar, and I sing."

"Would you sing for us today?"

"No, because I never do anything until I can do it properly."

"Well, you can choose if you listen or join in. But, class, would now be a good time to play some music?"

The children nod avidly.

Stacey stands to get his guitar and gives Joni a look of total relief.

Joni holds his eye contact and smiles endearingly at him with full respect.

Stacey puts the words for the song on the overhead projector and they shine onto the whiteboard.

"It's a song called 'Black and White'," he informs them.

"I remember this from my own school days," Joni tells them all.

Stacey smiles and begins to play. The class, except from Joe, all sing along. Joe is sat attentively although remains silent.

Jim walks in and pulls a face to Joni to show he is impressed with Stacey.

Joni nods with an expression to say she is very impressed with him.

She catches Stacey's eye and realises he has seen.

Near the end of the song, they sing 'together they grow to see the light, to see the light' and Joe stares at Joni, mouth open in amazement.

Joni laughs to herself in bemusement.

As Mr Polanski plays his last cord, Joni jumps to the front of the class.

"Let's give Mr Polanski a round of applause for his interesting answers and lovely song."

The children all clap for him with great enthusiasm and big smiles.

Stacey beams.

TWENTY

Joni is at the front of the class again, addressing the children.

"It's now our art lesson. We are each going to make a hat. We will firstly draw an insect using our learning from science and then make this into a hat."

Joni holds out a band with an extendable butterfly on it and puts it on her head.

"Here's one I made earlier. Mine is a butterfly but you can choose any insect."

The children look impressed at Joni's and excited at the thought of making one.

Stacey giggles to himself at her wearing the hat.

Clocking this, Joni raises her eyebrows at him in a jovial manner.

"I'm wearing this one so you can all see what you're aiming for. I'm now going to make one and then you're all going to make your own, so, it's important to watch and listen."

Kai puts his hand up.

Joni nods to him.

"Can Mr Polanski wear the one you're making?"

"Oh, it's for him," she informs them with a laugh.

The children all laugh. Stacey joins in.

The children are now in their places and fully engaged in making their hats. Joni and Stacey help the children to make them, each wearing an insect hat - Stacey's is a bumble bee.

Stacey is with Joe.

Joni walks over and overhears some of the conversation.

"It's my birthday next week," Joe tells him.

Stacey pulls a face to show excitement.

"And how old are you going to be?"

"Seven," he states as if it were obvious. "Everyone who has a birthday in this class will be seven."

"I remember being seven," Stacey reminisces. "It was fun."

Joe looks directly at Stacey.

"Being zero, and one, and two, and three, and four, and five, and six has not been fun, so I do hope so."

Stacey looks slightly taken back.

"I do hope so too for you."

Joe stares towards Stacey.

"Being six was the worst though because my grandad died."

Stacey smiles with deep empathy.

"I'm really sorry to hear that."

Stacey pauses, deep in thought.

"My grandad died when I was eight, so I know how tough it is. I spent a lot of time with him, so I missed him terribly."

"I miss my grandad," Joe tells him, his voice wobbling with emotion.

"It gets easier," Stacey attempts to console. He pauses and looks directly back at Joe.

"He'd be proud of you and how well you're doing at school."

Joe smiles at him. His face then wells up with tears.

"Are you okay?"

Joe breaks down, crying uncontrollably.

Joni walks over to him.

He looks up and sees her, throwing himself at her for a hug. Joni holds him whilst he cries.

Stacey looks over with concern, catching Joni's eye contact.

"I'm so sorry," he whispers to Joni. "I never meant to upset him."

Joni smiles empathetically to Stacey, seeing the genuine concern on his face. She continues to hold Joe as he deeply sobs.

"You didn't," she reassures. "You've been the best thing for him. This is what he needed to do."

Stacey smiles to accept.

Other children look over with concerned faces.

Joni holds Joe until he quietens down and pulls away.

He dries his eyes and composes himself.

"Can I carry on making my hat?"

Joni nods with an expression of kindness.

"With Mr Polanski?"

"Of course," she replies.

Joni smiles at Stacey with gratitude and respect.

"Come on Joe," he calls him back. "Where were we?"

Joe walks over to Stacey and whispers to him.

"If you do not have a wife, you could marry my teacher because she needs a husband."

Joni walks away, pretending to have not heard with an embarrassed, but amused, look on her face.

It is now home time, and the children all wait for their parents on the carpet with their coats on, holding their bags.

The children, Mrs Morton, Joni and Stacey are all wearing the hats they made.

"There's something I need to tell you all," Joni informs the class. "I'm on a course tomorrow so I'll be away, but I'll be back on Friday."

The children groan.

"Can Mr Polanski teach us?" asks Ethan.

"It won't be Mr Polanski," she replies.

The children groan again.

Most children have now left. Steph comes to the door and looks to Joni as if to ask how he has been. Joni gives her a thumbs up gesture and she smiles happily. Joni walks towards her.

"Just to let you know, I'm off tomorrow, on a course."

"Thanks for telling me," Steph smiles gratefully. "I'll go through it all tonight with Joe."

"I don't want to come tomorrow if you're not here," Joe shouts adamantly.

Joni turns to him.

"You are doing so well. Just carry on as you have been doing, and you'll be fine."

Joe studies her. His expression changes to sadness as he looks deep in thought.

"And you."

Joni looks puzzled.

"Me?"

"Yes, you," he repeats.

"Joe, you don't need to worry about me," Joni tells him, still perplexed.

Joe continues to study her.

"You will be fine," he continues.

He then nods towards Stacey.

"He's okay. He also has angels all around him."

Joni looks at him, unsure what to say.

Joe then gives her a big hug.

Joni hugs him back, touched by the gesture.

Steph smiles tenderly at her to see this.

"Come on Joe, you'll see Miss Nicholls on Friday. Say bye to Miss Nicholls."

"I don't want to say bye."

"Let's say, see you on Friday," Steph suggests to Joe.

Steph starts to walk off, holding Joe's hand.

Joe pulls her back but doesn't say anything.

"See you on Friday, Joe," Joni says to him.

Joe remains mute, just staring at her.

"See you on Friday, Miss Nicholls," Steph says and begins to walk off again. Joe walks with her this time, without saying anything. He looks back at her as he walks, long and hard, with a sad look in his eye.

Joni smiles at him.

He smiles a half smile back at her but turns a corner and is out of Joni's sight.

Joni stares ahead with an expression of confusion.

Mrs Morton walks over to Joni.

"I'll look after Joe tomorrow. You won't need to worry about him."

"Thank you. He won't like the change to his routine."

"I'll be here for him," Mrs Morton states to reassure her.

Joni looks at her with gratitude.

"I want you to know how much that means, and how much I appreciate all your support."

"I know you do," Mrs Morton replies. "That's why I love working for you."

Joni smiles warmly to her.

"Anyway, I'm off home now," she tells Joni. "I hope you enjoy your course tomorrow and have a good day," Mrs Morton adds. She then looks over to Stacey.

"He did well too. Especially with Joe. He seems a nice man."

Joni nods in agreement.

Mrs Morton pulls a face to suggest more.

Joni smiles again.

TWENTY-ONE

Joni walks over to Stacey with a mischievous smile.

"How was your 'easier' afternoon?"

Stacey laughs.

"I owe you an apology for my comment about the lower years being easier. I take my hat off to you."

Stacey takes the bumble bee hat from his head and laughs at the pun.

Joni laughs.

"Apology accepted. It's big of you to say. Hats off to you too."

Joni takes off her butterfly hat, also laughing at the pun.

"You're a natural. You did well and thank you for being that positive role model to the class."

Stacey smiles shyly.

"Anyway, I've a million things to do," she tells him dismissively. "So, all the best with your career. I believe you'll have a good one ahead of you."

Stacey doesn't leave but instead looks directly at her and bites his lip.

"Tomorrow is my last day, and, you're on a course, so, I won't see you again. So, I'm taking you out tonight to thank you for a wonderful afternoon. I'll meet you outside the wine bar just down the road at 7pm and, don't eat, I'll get dinner too. I'll see you then."

Stacey then leaves before Joni can speak.

She stands still in surprise.

Joni is now with Shirley on the sofa in Shirley's living room. They have cups in their hands and biscuits on the table.

"Have a biscuit," Shirley instructs her. "I thought they would be needed after your day."

Joni takes one.

"Thank you for your advice yesterday. It made all the difference today. It was a very rewarding day indeed."

Shirley beams to hear this.

"That's lovely to hear."

"We had some great discussions around it and the children showed great resilience."

"How was Joe?"

"He did well."

"His mum?"

"She thinks he predicted it. They all do. But we listened, and acknowledged, and they were happy for that."

"I'm so pleased to hear this."

"We'll never know if he did or didn't predict it. We just need to keeping building on the progress he has made."

Shirley nods to agree.

"So, the day you worried about turned out to be a good one?"

Joni pauses.

"The day was great, but…." she tails off.

Shirley pulls a face of interest.

"But?"

"Well, my day might not be over yet."

Shirley looks at her with intrigue.

"Why not?"

Joni giggles.

"The student turned out to be a man."

Shirley smirks with interest.

"A man has walked through your classroom?" she asks for confirmation.

"Yes."

"Tell me more about him."

"He was great with the children. They all loved him."

Joni pauses.

Shirley nods at her to continue.

"He's asked me out tonight."

"That's fantastic," Shirley replies.

"Well, he didn't ask. He told me to meet him and walked off!" Joni exclaims.

"And what would you have said?"

"No!"

Shirley looks at her, shaking her head.

"That's why he's done that. He knew you'd decline."

"I can't be dating my students."

Shirley shakes her head again.

"Anyway, why are you sat here with me?"

Joni looks directly at her but remains silent.

"Go and get yourself ready," Shirley commands.

"I'm still deciding whether to go."

Shirley rolls her eyes jovially but then turns to her with a serious expression.

"Go!"

"I haven't got any clothes that are suitable," Joni excuses.

Shirley frowns at her.

"I have to get up early tomorrow."

Shirley raises her eyebrows higher.

"I could be seen out with him by someone from school."

Shirley stares at her.

"Joni," she says to catch her focus. "You, my girl, are going," she tells her assertively.

They lock eyes.

Joni smiles with an expression to show she knows not to argue.

Joni walks up to the wine bar to see Stacey is already stood outside.

He smiles to see her coming.

"I'm so pleased you came," he greets her.

"I nearly didn't."

Stacey looks at her in bemusement.

"Imagine if someone from school sees us now."

"I was happy to risk it," he states.

"I'm sure you were," she states back jovially. "Me, not so."

Stacey smiles at her.

"Well, I'm very happy you came. Thank you. Hello, Joni."

"Yes, hello," she giggles.

Inside the wine bar, Joni and Stacey head over towards the bar. Stacey reaches into his pocket as they approach it.

"Tonight's on me but I've accidentally left my wallet in my car. It's right outside. Wait here, and I'll be straight back."

Joni nods at him.

He rushes towards the door.

Joni stands at the bar and looks up to a wine list on the wall, above the bar. She catches the eye of the barman and inaudibly whispers to him. They both laugh and he winks.

Stacey rushes back in.

"I'm sorry about that."

"No worries."

"What can I get you?" he asks.

"Just a Soave Classico for me, please, but they only sell it by the bottle, if that's okay?"

Stacey nods to her and turns to the barman.

"A Soave Classico and a coke, please."

"No problem," the barman replies. "That will be one hundred and thirty-two pounds, fifty pence, please."

"How much?" he instantly replies in shock.

Joni giggles whilst Stacey isn't looking.

The barman looks at him straight face.

"The coke is two pounds, and the Soave Classico is one hundred and thirty pounds and fifty pence. Will that be okay for you, Sir?"

Stacey turns to Joni who is now straight faced.

"It's a really nice wine."

Stacey stares at her, speechless.

Joni then laughs.

"A coke is good too."

"You had me worried for a moment there," laughs Stacey.

"It's not just six-year-olds with a high thought capacity. Twenty-six-year-olds can hold their own," she tells him, in a bantering style.

Stacey smiles, speechless.

"Mate," the barman says to grab Stacey's attention. "You'd better watch her," he jokes.

Stacey raises his eyes, in humour, to agree.

TWENTY-TWO

Joni and Stacey head to a table at the back of the wine bar, put their drinks down and pull out the chairs.

"What made you want to teach?" Joni asks him as she sits down.

"My best mate's parents were teachers," Stacey replies. "They were like a second family to me. They inspired me. I came from a single parent family where money was tight, so, at first, I wanted to make money, and I've been working in the city, but I didn't like it. I felt the calling to teach and here I am. What about you?"

"I bet they're proud of you for that," Joni smiles kindly as she speaks. "I always wanted to be a teacher. It's hard at times but I love it."

Stacey smiles warmly at her.

"I can tell. It shines through. You are a natural."

He then nods towards the pool table.

"Would you like to play in a bit?"

Joni looks over and shrugs her shoulders.

"We can do but you'll have to tell me how to play."

"I'd be happy to."

They are now both stood by the pool table, Stacey demonstrating how to play.

"Remember, when you take a shot, it's all about lining up the ball," Stacey instructs her, bending down to demonstrate. "You line the cue to hit the white ball at a point it will hit the colour at an angle to head off towards one of the pockets."

Joni nods at him.

"Do you want to start?" Stacey asks. "Or I can, to break the balls up."

"I can start," Joni replies blankly.

"Okay. You're sure?"

Joni nods.

"Aim for just off the centre of the front ball," Stacey tells her as he points to help her out.

Joni shows Stacey the cue.

"And you hold the cue like this?" she asks.

"Yes," Stacey answers. "That's good."

Joni smiles to him.

"Ready?" she asks.

"Ready."

Joni takes her shot and gets two red balls down.

"So, I'm red?" she asks blankly.

Stacey pauses in shock.

"Err. Yeah. You're red. That was a good shot."

"Thanks," she replies with a smile.

He looks at her with a frown of interest.

Joni then pots all the other red balls and lastly the black. Stacey stands motionless with his mouth open. The barman walks by.

"Nice one," he compliments to Joni.

"I said to watch her," he says to Stacey.

Stacey pulls an expression to the barman to agree.

"I didn't even get a go!"

"I did say you were a natural teacher," Joni jovially tells him.

"I'm guessing you've played several times before and I've been hustled."

Joni looks at him flirtatiously.

"Did you think 'I' would be 'easy'?" she teases.

Stacey laughs.

"I'm thinking nothing about you is going to be easy."

Joni nods to agree with a giggle. She heads back to their table and Stacey follows her.

"Where did you learn to play like that?" he asks as he sits down.

"My dad."

Stacey looks at her to continue.

"He was in a league. I still have his pool table from their home in my flat so play often."

"Wow."

"I lost both my parents," Joni confides in him.

"I'm sorry to hear. How long ago?"

"It was seven years ago now. Six months apart from each other. There were better years."

"You've looked after yourself since?"

Joni nods.

Stacey smiles affectionately, glancing at her with interest.

They are now in an Indian restaurant with many dishes in front of them.

"You thought they'd eat me alive, didn't you?"

Joni giggles.

"There was a point I thought they were going to win, but you came back strong and took them on."

Joni takes a bite, screams, spits out her food and gulps her water.

Stacey looks at her with shock.

"Oh, my. Are you okay? What has happened?"

"There's something wrong with that runner bean."

Stacey looks at it and starts to laugh.

"That's not a runner bean. That's a chilli pepper."

"A chilli pepper?"

Stacey laughs again.

Joni throws him a look.

"I usually eat quite plainly," she says through heavy breathing.

Stacey giggles.

Joni tries to hold back a smile.

"Do I see a laugh?" jests Stacey. "Are you starting to see the funny side?"

Joni laughs.

"Maybe it's karma," Stacey states. "For the expensive drink trick and seven balling me. Karma in the form of a runner bean."

They look at each other and laugh.

Joni and Stacey leave the restaurant.

"I can drop you back home," he suggests. "I came by car."

"Thank you," she replies with a sincerity. "But no. I'll get a cab."

"Okay, but I'll walk you to the taxi rank and make sure you get in safely."

"I appreciate that."

They start to walk to the taxi rank.

"When can I next see you?" Stacey asks.

"You're always very presumptuous," she says kindly.

"I'm scared you'll say 'no'. Can we meet again?"

"We can't meet again. I'm sorry," she says with genuine regret.

"Today is a day I'm never going to forget. I'd like to see you again."

"I can't. I'm sorry."

Stacey stops. He looks at Joni, dejected, but nods in acceptance. He then walks on again and they walk in silence.

Stacey knocks on a door of a cab at the rank. The taxi driver winds down his window.

"Do you have a pen and a card, mate?"

The taxi driver fumbles but hands them to him. Stacey writes on the back of the card and hands the pen back to the cab driver.

"Thanks, mate."

Stacey turns to Joni.

"Here's my number."

Stacey hands the card to Joni.

She takes it with a smile.

Stacey looks at her with a serious expression.

"I don't want to put on you here but if you ever want to go for another night out, do call."

Joni looks at him apologetically.

"I have never met anyone before that I would like to meet again as much as I would like to meet you again," he tells her. "We can avoid chilli peppers."

Joni laughs.

"I'm sorry, but I can't."

Stacey nods to accept and smiles at her.

"Thank you for the drinks and meal. I did have a lovely time," she tells him but then gets into the cab.

Stacey gently closes the door behind her.

The cab driver starts up the engine and pulls off.

Stacey waves as she leaves.

She waves back.

Inside the cab, Joni watches from the window as Stacey fades into the distance. He is stood, watching the cab drive off.

She turns back around, looks at the card and sighs.

TWENTY-THREE

Joni, Stacey, Jake and Luke remain at the kitchen table.

"The day I met your mother is one I'll never forget," Stacey tells them.

"So, you also taught Joe Huckle?" Luke asks.

"Just for that afternoon."

"And we're here because of Joe Huckle suggesting to you to marry mum. That's crazy."

"Sort of," laughs Stacey. "I fell for your mum."

"I admit I'd have never got back in touch with him without the Huckles. Oh, and Shirley," Joni adds.

"How was Shirley when you saw her last week?" Stacey deviates. "I meant to ask."

"Still doing well. Planning her ninetieth birthday party."

Joni smiles at the thought.

"What did the Huckles do to get you back in touch with Dad?" asks an intrigued Jake.

Luke stares on in interest.

Later, Joni returns to her spare room, opens her diary and turns to the diary page headed: 'Thursday 13th September 2001'.

2001

Joni is on her sofa and stares ahead, deep in thought. There is a knock at the door. She sighs and gets up to answer.

Joni opens the door to see Shirley.

"Well, how was last night?" she asks with keen anticipation.

Joni leads Shirley to her living room and sits down. Shirley joins her.

"Last night seems ages ago. I've been on a course all day. But, yes, I had a great time."

"I'm so pleased for you. I was thinking of you all night. When are you next seeing him?"

Joni looks at her blankly.

"I'm not."

Shirley looks saddened.

"Did he not ask to see you again?"

"He did, but I said no," Joni replies directly.

"Why?"

Joni pauses with a face to show she's made up her mind.

"I don't want my life to change. Before you ask why, I'm happy as I am. It was fun but, I'm not seeing him again."

Shirley looks at Joni in exasperation.

"And when is a man next going to just walk through your classroom? I can answer that. Never. Never, Joni. Give him one more chance."

Joni shrugs her shoulders.

"If you never go, you'll never know. When you get to my age you only regret what you didn't do."

Joni stares blankly.

"I've made up my mind."

Shirley studies her, disappointed for her.

"I know you fear the pain of loss again, but you'll never find happiness," Shirley whispers and smiles with a genuine concern for her.

Joni looks up, realising she understands her. She smiles at Shirley for her concern.

"Your hat was a butterfly," Shirley adds. "It was a symbol that it's time to be brave. Time to fly from your cocoon."

Joni looks down, speechless but deep in thought.

2021

Joni is in her kitchen, watching the news about the twentieth anniversary of 9/11 approaching tomorrow. She hears how the Queen has planned a speech to mark the occasion, as well as a ceremony planned in the US.

"Twenty years," she says nostalgically under her breath.

Joni heads back to her spare room. She pauses to look out of the window. Then, with a smile, she turns the page to that headed: 'Friday 14th September 2001'.

2001

Joni walks through the school staff entrance to be met by Jim, having waited for her.

"Hi," she says as she sees him.

"Joni, can you pop into my office with me?" he asks with a very serious expression.

Joni nods, an expression of growing concern.

He walks off and she follows apprehensively.

Now entering his office, Jim holds the door open for her.

Joni takes a chair and sits down, looking at him, eyes wide.

Jim closes the door behind them and takes a seat. He gathers his thoughts before he speaks, looking to Joni with sadness in his eyes.

Joni glares at him in concern.

He looks up but remains quiet.

"Was everything okay yesterday with the supply teacher?" she asks to break the silence.

"It wasn't an easy day. I need to update you."

"Was everything okay with Joe?"

Jim stares directly at her and then shakes his head.

"What did Joe do?" she asks.

"Joe wasn't there," he replies.

Joni frowns in confusion.

"Oh. He was absent?"

"Joni, I'm so sorry to tell you this but Joe has left."

"Left?" Joni questions in shock.

"Yes, he's left this school. I know how involved you've become, and this is a shock, but they've moved away."

"Moved? When?"

"They left yesterday."

Joni pauses in shock.

Jim looks at her with deep empathy.

"What? They didn't mention this on Wednesday."

"They didn't know on Wednesday. They had to leave very suddenly Wednesday evening."

Joni looks confused.

"Yesterday morning, his mum came to see me just before they left. She came alone. You wouldn't have seen Joe anyway, even if you'd been here. He was already in hiding."

Joni is silent, still in shock.

"The details are confidential. All I can say is there was an incident at their house. Joe's father didn't react well to the premonition. An argument turned into a fight, and he hurt her. Quite badly. Noah defended his mum but got hurt too. Noah is in hospital."

"What?" Joni stutters. "Noah is in hospital." Joni's eye well up with tears to hear this.

"Whilst the dad was being held at the police station for questioning, she packed quickly and left with Joe. She wouldn't say where she was going. She admitted he can get rough with her, but she won't stand for it with her child."

"No," is all Joni can manage as a tear rolls down her cheek.

"Noah will join them on his release."

"Was he badly hurt?" she asks, trying to compose herself.

"I don't know."

Joni stares ahead, speechless.

"This has hit me hard too. It's hard to detach yourself but you must."

Joni breaks down and sobs.

Jim takes off his glasses and sighs as he watches her.

"I'm going to ask you to take the rest of the day off," he instructs her.

Joni shakes her head.

Jim pulls a face to suggest he won't change his mind.

"You've never had a day off. You need to be one hundred percent for your class. You are taking today and will be ready to start again on Monday."

Joni nods to accept.

Jim passes her a tissue. She takes it, nods again and wipes her eyes.

Jim gets a gift bag from under his desk.

"His mum left a little gift to pass to you," Jim tells her as he hands her the bag. "She wanted to say how she will never forget you and how you made the difference for Joe."

Joni takes the gift bag. It is sealed.

"Open it at home," he tells her.

Joni takes it, touched by this gesture.

"In all of that, she thought of me?"

Jim nods with a big smile.

"You're a great teacher, Joni. One of the best."

Joni stares ahead, speechless.

"Look after yourself this weekend. I'll see you on Monday."

TWENTY-FOUR

Joni enters her flat and walks over to her couch. She sits, with her coat still on, and places her bag and gift bag next to her. She picks up the gift bag, opens it and pulls out a card in a child's writing. She reads it to herself.

> *To Miss Nicholls,*
>
> *I wanted to write because I can write now. You will be the first person to see my writing. I am sorry I had to go. I will miss you very much. Thank you for teaching me and being kind to me. Don't worry about me. I'm going to try hard to be good at my next school. Don't forget me. Don't be afraid and take a chance too.*
>
> *From Indigo Joe.*

Joni opens the bag again and inside is a CD of 'Joni Mitchell's Greatest Hits'. She turns it over and there is a message on a note stuck to the back in an adult's writing.

> *We will never forget you. You changed everything for Jonah. Thank you deeply. Play 'Woodstock'. It always reminds me of Jonah.*

Joni gets up and puts the CD on, to play 'Woodstock'. She stares out of her window as it plays, listening to all the lyrics that feel so applicable to her. On hearing, 'I dreamed I saw the bombers riding shot gun in the sky, and they were turning into butterflies', she pauses it.

She then looks around her flat and picks up a picture of her with her parents, fighting emotion. She then sighs, breathes in and breaks down.

On composing herself, she then picks up the cab card with Stacey's number on it. She picks up her phone, goes to dial but puts it down. She then dials. It rings and is answered.

"Hello," says Stacey's voice from the phone.

"Hi, it's Joni," she says with a wobbly voice and expression of shock towards herself for doing this.

"Joni. Hi. It's great to hear from you. Are you not at work today?"

"I went in, but I got sent home."

"Are you ill?" Stacey asks in concern.

"I'm not ill. I was upset."

"Upset?" he questions.

"I came back in this morning, after my course yesterday, to find out that Joe has left. I called because I thought you may want to know."

"I do want to know. Thank you for calling to tell me. This is a shock. Is he okay?"

"I'm not sure."

"Is he coming back?"

"No. He's not."

"I'm so sorry to hear that. I'm only studying, and it can wait. We can meet at the wine bar for lunch if you would like to? You have a friend."

"I'd like a friend. The wine bar is good. Twelve o'clock?"

"Twelve o'clock."

"No runner beans," Joni laughs.

"No pool," Stacey laughs.

"We have a deal."

They both laugh.

"We have a deal," he tells her affectionately. "See you then."

"See you then."

Joni closes the call and smiles to herself.

Joni leaves her flat and passes Shirley entering hers. She is shocked to see Joni.

"Joni. Not at school?"

"Oh, Shirley. It's a long story. I can't stop. I'll pop in tonight to tell you."

"Are you okay?"

"No. Joe left. I got sent home for being upset and I'm now off to meet my student again."

Shirley's eyes widen with happiness.

"Skipping school and meeting men," Shirley teases humorously. "Do pop in later."

"When you put it like that!" Joni laughs.

"Take care, Joni, and I'll see you later," Shirley tells her with a caring concern. "Have a good time," she adds.

Shirley walks into her flat.

"Shirley," Joni shouts back for her.

Shirley turns around and waits for her to speak.

"I think a child just taught me something."

Shirley smiles with a wisdom.

Joni and Stacey are at the bar and the same barman comes over.

"Hello, again. What can I get you?"

"The Soave Classico and two glasses," Stacey answers.

Joni stares at him in shock.

"No. That was a joke before."

"Yes, as long as you do actually like a wine at lunchtime?"

"I'd love a wine but a cheaper bottle."

Stacey turns to the barman.

"The Soave Classico and two glasses," he repeats.

"For real this time?" the barman asks.

Stacey nods to the barman. He then smiles lovingly at Joni.

She thinks of Joe's 'communication through illustration', and how he said it can extend beyond drawing. She smiles back at him, touched by his gesture.

"I owe you a crystal for Monday," Stacey states. "We can shop after lunch if you'd like?"

"Thank you," Joni laughs. "I'd love to."

Stacey stares in shock at this response but beams a big smile at her.

2021

Joni, Stacey, Jake and Luke remain at the kitchen table.

"It's honestly never been a dull moment from the afternoon I walked into her classroom," Stacey tells Jake and Luke.

"Why do you not teach anymore?" Jake asks his mum.

"Teaching changed. It became increasingly about the results."

"Oh, don't I know," laughs Jake.

"But, not only did teaching change, so did I, and I wanted to help children in difficult situations so that's when I retrained as a social worker, after having you two."

"To me it's more important than ever to be a good teacher," Stacey states. "It's a hard job so I support my teachers the best I can."

"Boys, your dad was a natural," Joni tells them. "He had a gift. That's why he rose to the top quickly."

Joni smiles proudly at him.

"He's loved by his staff," she continues. "A true example of how a head should be."

Stacey and Joni smile at each other.

"Did you ever hear of Joe again?" Jake questions.

"Not until now. To think, it was Joe who taught me to take a chance on life."

"Joe taught you that?" Luke asks doubtfully.

They all look up to the television. Joe screams into the microphone as part of a song. Luke raises his eyebrows, even more doubtful. Joni, Stacey and Jake laugh.

"Shall we all go out for a pizza?" Stacey suggests.

"I'm going to Max's tonight for a guitar session and dinner," replies Jake.

"Aiden's mum said I could go to his for dinner tonight before football," answers Luke.

"They had both already been arranged," Joni informs Stacey.

"If it's just us, do you want to go out to celebrate the success of Jonah Huckle?" Stacey suggests. "And twenty years of us! There is still a nice little wine bar in town."

"Why not?" answers Joni. "But no runner beans."

"No pool," replies Stacey.

"A bottle of Soave Classico?" laughs Joni.

"Why not?" laughs Stacey.

Jake and Luke look at each other and roll their eyes.

"Here's Indigo Joe when they played a cover of a Joni Mitchell song," interrupts Jake, getting it up on YouTube. "It went viral in America and then the world. You may like it, also being called Joni."

Joni looks directly at Jake with interest. She turns to Stacey who is also looks intrigued.

Jake puts the performance on the television. The audience is cheering for Joe. He smiles in gratitude as he waits for it to be quiet enough to speak.

"A message to our growing number of followers," Joe tells the audience. "Be yourself, follow your heart and be afraid of neither."

The audience cheers again. Joe waits again for quiet and smiles as he does.

"This next song is a 'Joni Mitchell' classic. It reminds me of a special teacher from when I was young and who I sing this for today."

He begins to sing 'Woodstock' in his own gripping and haunting style.

Joni and Stacey look at each other in total surprise.

Joni then walks over to the window. The crystal is hanging, and it splits the light. She puts her hand to her mouth and fights tears. She smiles as she hears the voice of her younger self: "Just be yourself, Joe. Follow your heart. Never be afraid to do either."

Stacey walks over and takes her hand. They smile tenderly to each other and then both look up at the television screen as Indigo Joe sing the rest of 'Woodstock'.

Printed in Dunstable, United Kingdom